Blessing

OUTSIDE THE

LINES

Bleeding Outside the Lines is an adult dark romance novel intended for ages 18+. This book contains graphic language and content that some readers may find distressing, including sexual themes, abuse, and torture.

For a full list of content warnings please visit:
jessallenauthor.com/#trigger-warnings

For anyone who has ever made the wrong move,

and still won the game.

Bleeding

OUTSIDE THE

LINES

JESS ALLEN

PLAYLIST

Ride – SoMo
Fucked Up, Kinda – Julia Michaels
I Hate Everything About You – Three Days Grace
Too Close – Alex Clare
FMRN – Lilyisthatyou
River – Bishop Briggs
Do I Wanna Know? – Arctic Monkeys
Blood in the Water – Joanna Jones as The Dame
Paint It, Black – Ciara
Young God – Halsey
Love on the Brain – Rihanna
Teeth – 5 Seconds of Summer
Crazy Bitch – Buckcherry
Slave – Fyval Winter, Theo Riot
I Get Off – Halestorm
Suga Boom Boom – Down3r
Hot Dog – Limp Bizkit
cinderella's dead – EMELINE

Gorgeous Gorgeous Girls – Lilyisthatyou
rapunzel – emlyn
Wicked as They Come – CRMNL
Bird of Prey – Emily James
In My Head – Taylor Acorn
Bloodline – Natalie Jane
When Worlds Collide – Powerman 5000
Titanium – David Guetta feat. Sia
Coming Undone – Korn
Big Bad Wolf – Roses & Revolutions
Control – Halsey
Angels On The Moon – Thriving Ivory
If You Want Love – NF
You Put A Spell On Me – Austin Giorgio
The Sound of Silence – Disturbed
Dark Side – Iris Grey
Brand New Numb – Motionless In White
Come For Me – New Years Day
Soulmate – Chanin
Training Season – Dua Lipa
Make You Mine – Madison Beer
I Am Above – In Flames

ONE

Her tongue darts out, catching the drop of cum that dribbled out of her mouth. She shifts her gaze, and her big brown eyes look up at me from where she kneels on the floor, young and eager. I quickly stuff my cock back into the confines of my pants before it gets any more ideas. Annoyed that my body is still stiff in every other way, I massage my temples. I keep thinking that this is the answer to releasing the cords that wind me up, but all it does is frustrate me more. Apparently, orgasms are not what the doctor ordered.

A lesser man might turn to drugs to scratch the unscratchable itch, but I am not a lesser man. One might say that using women makes me a lesser man, but I dare them to say that to my fucking face. People have died for less.

"Clean up and forget you were in here," I bark at the girl still kneeling expectantly in front of me. A pout distorts her pretty face, but she doesn't say a word, pulling at the hem of her skirt as she stands. Her cleavage spills over the neckline of her shirt, and her tits scream at me, begging to be fucked. I huff, disinterested and push my office door shut behind her, seconds later the electronic lock mechanism beeps. Metal scratches on metal as the deadbolts rotate into place.

Fuck me. I unzip my pants and settle into my chair, my legs propped wide. My dick is hard again, and I grip it tight. My hand glides easily up and down my shaft, still slick with her saliva. What I wouldn't give to be between her tits right now, my tip grazing her lips with every thrust. I have been insatiable lately. My balls are their own shade of blue, regardless of how many times I get my dick wet. None of these bar bunnies have been enough. But it's hard to know what's enough when you don't know what you crave. I thought it was sex, but based on my escapades recently, I think it's safe to say that's just a cover story. A life of dirty money and blurred lines makes it easy to lie to myself.

Pushing my frustration aside, I tighten my grip, desperate for relief. The smell of the bar bunny lingers in the air, sweet and spicy. I picture her big brown eyes looking up at me as I fucked her mouth.

Fuck her eyes. They watered as she took my full length, but she never backed down, never once pulled back. My dick throbs in my hand with every stroke as I think about her hard nipples playing peek-a-boo in her barely-there shirt. I find one of my own nipples beneath my shirt and pinch it to the point of pain.

I'm right on the edge, teetering on that fine line between pleasure and needing more. But more what? I release my grip on my cock.

"Fuck!" My voice booms in the empty room. Rolling my shoulders, I take a deep breath and then fist myself again. I thrust my hips, fucking my hand harder than is usually necessary, and pinch my nipple again. My hand glides up and down my shaft. Up. Down. Tighter. Faster.

Fuck her pouty lips that left a pink lipstick ring on my cock.

Fuck.

A light throbbing starts in my balls before they tighten, and I shoot my load all over my empty desk, continuing to pump my cock until the last drop dribbles down my fist.

It's not until I reach for a towel to clean up that I see the problem. My desk isn't empty. Right in the middle, now coated in my cum, is a small red envelope that wasn't there before. I grab the towel out of my desk drawer and make quick work of wiping off my hand and then the envelope without bothering with the desk. Once again, I tuck my cock safely back into the confines of my pants.

I don't need to see the black wax seal on the back of her signature red envelope to know who it's from. With a hesitant hand, I grab my knife from my pocket. I stare at my last name, Cross, in neat script on the front of the envelope for what feels like hours.

Who does this bitch think she is? And worse ... who had the balls to hire her?

I slide the knife into the envelope, tear it open, and pull out the cream-colored paper. Red filigree adorns the edges, and swirly black script fills the page. A blood-red signature sits at the bottom.

They say she's a ghost. That she hides among the shadows. Nobody knows what she looks like, yet everyone knows who she is. She's a master of disguise, with no age and no heart. They say that a letter from her is an instant death sentence. Anger works its way up my spine and settles in my chest. The letter crumples in my tightened fist.

Fuck that dumb bitch. I pull a tablet out of my desk drawer and turn on the video feed for the bar. Sitting directly in front of the camera is the woman who was just on her knees, worshiping my cock. Her tits rest on the bar while her eyes taunt me through the screen.

Her lips are painted a bright shade of red, no longer the sorority girl pink she wore in my office. They lift into a triumphant smile before she plucks the cherry out of her drink and passes it through her freshly painted lips, stem and all.

Determined to catch her before she leaves, I stand, shoving the unread letter in my pocket. I quickly turn the levers to slide the deadbolts out of place before barreling through the door, pulling it closed behind me. I take the stairs two at a time, down to the bar. The stool sits empty; only a knotted cherry stem remains as proof she was ever really there. I don't know if I want to put a bullet through her skull or spank her ass until she apologizes for not swirling her tongue on my dick like that. I repeat, *fuck this bitch.*

I scan the rest of the bar, but it's pointless. She's gone.

"Move," I yell, pressing into the crowd of bodies, shoving dancing men and women out of my path. "Get out of my fucking way."

Above me, strobe lights flash and the bass from the music pounds through me, matching my anger. *Motherfucker.* I am too far away to catch up with her, the bodies in the bar growing thicker, sweatier, and more defiant. But I continue pushing against the crowd, forcing my way through.

I reach the edge of the dance floor, and there she is, her back to me, standing at the exit.

"Stop her!" I shout to my bouncer, but he must not hear me over the music because he doesn't move. As if sensing my presence, she turns her head, and her eyes find mine. I'm still too far away. I reach for my gun. I should shoot her between the eyes right here, but I can't in this crowd of people.

Her fingers touch her red lips, and she blows me a kiss before walking out of my club.

The kiss of death.

I don't know what's worse, knowing someone wants you dead and not knowing who it is, or being turned on by the prospect of going toe to toe with the queen herself. The world spins around me, but my feet are planted firmly on the ground. Energy pulses through my veins, and every hair on my arms stands up. Even the colors are brighter. It feels like the ultimate high, like I'm alive for the first time in months. It's ironic, really.

I force myself to move. I have things to accomplish. I cannot stand here while she's out there. I have a bitch to kill. I am Cassius fucking Cross. I destroy anyone who threatens me. I've worked too hard and too long to get here. I push bodies out of my way, voices of protest following in my wake.

Again, I take the stairs two at a time, my long legs barely

straining. The door to my office is open, which is impossible because I know I fucking closed it.

"Come out, come out wherever you are," I pull my gun from its holster before I enter, ready and willing to shoot a bitch between the eyes. She's not fucking here, but somebody was, and I slam the door behind me, hearing it lock.

"Stupid fucking slut!" My foot connects with the trash barrel, sending its contents across the floor. Picking up the chair in front of my desk, I hurl it at the wall. It hits with a thump, leaving a hole in the sheetrock, but the chair falls back to the ground unharmed. I pick it up again, this time throwing it at the bar cart. Bottles of liquor and glasses fall to the floor with thuds and crashes.

I crack my neck and lean over to pick up a tequila bottle, broken at the neck, but still partially full. Digging through the debris, I also find a shot glass mostly intact, except for the small chip in the rim.

I pour myself a shot, appreciating the sting as it burns its way down my throat, and sit behind my desk. Picking up my tablet, I tap on the camera feed from my office, rewinding it an hour and lean back in my chair, confident that I have achieved what every person before me has failed, capturing this cunt on camera. As an added perk, I can watch her sucking my cock whenever the mood strikes. An audible laugh escapes me, and I watch the screen as the door to my office opens, revealing me behind it. Then it happens again. And again. I fast-forward and watch as the door opens on a loop for twenty fucking minutes. And then I am shooting my load on my desk and picking up the envelope.

Motherfucking bitch.

I refill my shot glass and then switch over to the bar camera. Again, I rewind the feed. Again, she's never there, but when I zoom in, the cherry stem sits on the napkin. I know it's pointless to look, but I follow suit with the rest of the video feeds anyway. The feed from behind the DJ booth that shows the dance floor, the feed at the door, and the feed in the hallway. All of them, empty of the brunette. What remains of the tequila bottle smashes against the wall.

I need the night to get my head straight, and I can't do it here. I can't think without seeing her on her fucking knees. I leave through the back exit and climb into the driver's seat of my rebuilt Impala. My feet press down on the clutch and brake, and I turn the key. She purrs to life. My cock does a little bounce in greeting. I bought this car as a bucket of rust and used the money I won from my first big card game to rebuild it. Every time I turn her on, it's like losing my virginity all over again. I pull out of the lot, the power beneath me feeding the tension in my body.

I'm not worried about this bitch killing me. Truly, I'm not. She hides in the shadows, beneath disguise and fancy fanfare. I own who I am. People fear me, not the idea of me. I am a tangible, real-life person. She's a rumor. A hushed conversation in a dark corner. But fuck me if she doesn't have me all revved up.

I need to know who the fuck hired her and why. I stick to my own corner of the darkness that lurks beneath this city. You won't find me running drugs or pimping out women. You won't even find me buying drugs or sex. Gambling is my vice. I learned how to count cards as a kid, and by the time I was twenty-four, I had opened the club, but only as a cover for the underground micro-casino. My vice turned into a million-dollar business. We have high-stakes poker, blackjack, and a few craps tables. It's invite or referral only. I don't have goons. I handle my own shit. You fuck me over, and you face me—or the end of my fist, or maybe my trusty hammer. And if it's still not handled, you go missing and stay missing.

I rack my brain, trying to think of who would be brave or stupid enough to hire this woman. And who has the funds? The pricks that run the drug and sex trades aren't this stupid. And it can't possibly be anyone who owes me money, because if they have the funds to pay this bitch, they have the funds to pay me, making killing me pointless.

I punch the code and drive through the gate and up the long driveway to my home. It sits on a little over seven acres right outside the city and is surrounded by an eight-foot stockade fence armed with monitored cameras. It screams *nobody fucks with Cassius Cross*. I pull the Impala into the garage, head into the house, and make my way to the bar.

I pour a few shots of tequila over ice and get comfortable in my home office. The letter that weighed heavy in my pocket for the last hour now sits crumpled in front of me. I smooth it as best I can on the surface of my desk.

Dear Mr. Cross,

Death. The permanent ending.

Unless of course you believe in the afterlife.

However, if you believe in such a thing, you may want to reconsider. Perhaps if you do not believe in hell, then one would not exist for you to enter. By now, you know I have been hired to kill you – a job I take very seriously. If the rumors about you are true, then I anticipate a formidable opponent.

Let the hunt begin,

Ruby

I stare at the letter, reading it over and over. Memorizing it. I have so many questions and no answers. But I do know one thing for sure, I'm not going down without a fight. In fact, if anyone goes down, it's going to be her.

On her fucking knees. Again.

Two

The phone barely has a chance to ring before he answers.

"Cross," his deep voice greets me across the airwaves. It's surprising that he answered on the first ring. Perhaps this job will be easier than anticipated.

"Good evening, Cassius," I reply, my voice a soft purr. "May I call you Cassius? Mr. Cross seems far too professional for such an intimate relationship." I watch the video feed in front of me, as the man I have been paid to kill sits unmoving. Not a twitch in his armor. His eyes are cold and gray. They seem to see everything but look at nothing.

His tongue slides across his lips before my name spills out of his mouth. "Ruby." It falls in the air fluid like the rain outside my window. He remains still as a statue, as if he'll die if he so much as breathes. As if he knows I am watching him. Can he feel my gaze on him?

"I must say," he continues. "I'm slightly disappointed in your skills tonight."

"I assure you, Cassius, I am the best at what I do. Be grateful you still draw breath."

His silence speaks volumes, louder than any heartbeat. Louder than the quickened breath of the afraid. Silence is all the reassurance I need to know that I have him exactly where I want him.

Predator vs. prey.

"Now, Cassius, here is what's going to happen." I drop my voice an octave, each syllable drips of sex, raw and sultry. This is part of the game, part of the hunt. "I am going to kill you, but you will not know when, and you will not know how. You will not see me coming, but you will know when I am near."

From the bar in my office, I pour myself a glass of wine and then sink into the cushioned chair behind my desk, kicking off my heels. The wine is bitter, coating my throat with hints of plum and cherry. It's not my favorite, but it was sent to me from Spain, so I drink it anyway.

The statue on the screen moves. He relaxes in his chair, propping his feet on the desk. Interesting. Peculiar even. It's as if he sees my death threat as an invitation. This catches me off guard, increasing my heart rate. I feel every pulse through my veins, betraying my normal calm demeanor.

What the hell is this man doing?

My breath hitches and I pull the phone away, hoping he didn't notice.

"Baby, I understand that you were hired to do a job, but you're setting yourself up for failure."

"Call me baby again, and I will gut your insides and feed them to the vermin that haunt the alley behind your club."

"Not if I gut you first. I suggest you crawl back to whoever the fuck hired you and tell them there has been a change of plans. Tell them that you won't be killing me because you tasted my dick, and it's like a drug you can't kick."

A click sounds in my ear, followed by deafening silence. He hung up. The piece of shit actually hung up on me. Ruby. The Ruby. The motherfucking queen. My wine glass shatters against the wall, and I find the sound it makes oddly comforting. Sweet like music but like life, gone so quick. Adrenaline courses through my veins. Splatters of deep red coat the walls, cautioning what's to come.

Careful to step around the glass in my bare feet, I exit my office and walk up the steep stairs to the top floor of the house. Every criminal mastermind has an antisocial man in his basement that sits behind the computer; mine just happens to be a woman in an attic. She is quite like Rapunzel, except Rowan has short, curly, brown hair, and she's not locked in, but rather I am locked out. And while she is not a long-lost princess, she was once a lost little girl. We all were.

The red light from the scanner searches my wrist. When it finds the chip embedded in my skin, a beep sounds, and the door opens. Rowan does not acknowledge my presence. Her fingers, fast from years of practice, continue to tap at the keyboard in front of her.

"Earth to Rowan." I wave a hand in front of her. She blinks rapidly at the intrusion, her eyes large behind her glasses.

"Dude," she screams loud enough to wake the rest of the house.

"Dude," I mimic and point to her noise-canceling headphones.

Her curls bounce as she laughs, and she slings the headphones around her neck.

"Did you get a chance to review the information the client provided?" I ask, pacing behind her.

Her nose scrunches and releases over and over again. I give her a moment, because trying to rush her or getting frustrated with her will only make it last longer. When her face finally relaxes, I lift my hand to stop her before the inevitable apology can leave her lips.

She inhales deeply. "You know what he did doesn't matter, right? Like we were contracted for a job, and this is not actually part of it."

"But she could be any one of us, Row. We have to find her."

Her shoulders push back, and her chin lifts. She has resigned herself to the second part of this. The part we are not getting paid for. The part the police can't seem to solve.

"It's legit, Rubes. Like a hundred percent. Did you actually tell him what you knew?"

"No, you know me. I have to play with him first, like a new toy."

"Is that why you licked his toy like a lollipop?" Rowan giggles, but I don't join in her amusement. She knows I would if I could.

"Did you see him? I may be a monster, but I'm still

a woman. I have needs. And if those needs just happen to help me with a mark who looks like Mr. Cross, I'm going to take full advantage." I speak the truth; Cassius is a unique specimen. His golden-brown complexion combined with his eyes, gray like a storm cloud, are devastating. The way he moved around his club dripping sex appeal before our rendezvous—purely intoxicating. Every time he brushed his thumb across the scruff on his chin, I imagined what it would feel like between my legs. But later, when he saw the barstool empty and stalked after me ... that moment holds me in its clutches. The challenge in his eyes when I blew him the kiss. The clench of his jaw, the tightening of his fist. He exuded power, even when he had none.

"That was superb work with the video feed, by the way," I tell her, because without it, Cassius would have my face on camera, and I can't have that.

"I'm feeling the brunette Rubes. You got lucky he didn't pull your hair."

I flick my hand to wave off her comment. "I wasn't worried. Rayna has this thing on so tight, it could survive a hurricane. Speaking of which, I have to go take this thing off before my scalp rebels and I have to shave my head."

I turn to leave, but Rowan speaks again, stopping me in my tracks. Her voice is barely a whisper over the whirring of the computers.

"Do you ever miss it?" Rowan asks.

"Miss what?"

"Seeing yourself when you look in the mirror?"

If anyone else asked me this question, my answer would be simple. No. But sometimes I think Rowan knows me better than I know myself. She is the one who held my hand when the expectations were heavier than I could handle. Her kindness kept me anchored when I wanted nothing more than to drift away. So instead, I answer her honestly.

"It's hard to miss something that was never really there." I squeeze her shoulder gently, "See you in the morning Row, get some sleep." Closing the attic door behind me, I climb down the stairs to the first floor, where my suite is. The house is quiet, which is not unusual. Everyone is in bed.

The stories are true, I'm a chameleon. We all have to be. It's part of the assassin job description. My research, or rather Rowan's, had been thorough on Cassius. I was exactly who I needed to be tonight to gain access to his private office. Could I have done it without the invitation? Of course. I didn't earn my reputation for nothing. But I like to play with my prey before I pounce.

Sitting at the vanity in my room, I gently remove the wig. Long, red hair falls down my back. I place the wig on the designated hook on the wall; not a hair out of place on it. I remove the brown contacts from my eyes, and jade green ones look back at me. I stare at the woman in the mirror, Rowan's words haunting me. Closing my eyes, I count to three, hopeful that when I open them, the mirror will reveal a different face—one I might recognize. But hope is a blade on which to fall, and this time the stranger looks back at me with a tear in her eye.

Blinking rapidly, I detach myself from the moment. I collapse into bed and pull up Cassius' video feed on my phone, watching him sleep. It would be so easy to climb into his window and slit his throat while he dreams. Easy, but not fun. With the press of a button, I set off every alarm on his property.

Cassius startles awake and immediately reaches for his nightstand. Suddenly the room is filled with light and Cassius climbs out of bed, his naked body filling my screen. He lifts a gun into the empty air, then looks off camera. I can't tell what he's looking at, but his chest heaves and his nostrils flare. My breath catches in my throat as the lamplight ripples over his body with every move he makes. I thought his eyes were intoxicating, but I was wrong. It's his tight ass that I can't take my eyes off of as he walks into the bathroom. He emerges with a tablet in hand and his dick, soft but still impressive, swinging back and forth like a pendulum, hypnotizing me with its girth. Until, as if I willed it to happen, it hardens like stone. The absence of alarm sirens breaks my trance, and I watch as his shoulders roll with the kind of tension I know so well. Energy. So much energy. The same kind of energy I can feel in the tips of my fingers. His tablet falls to the bed, and his hand wraps around his cock.

I want to watch, but it is against protocol. A protocol that was put into place long before my reign. So instead, I shut down my phone and bury myself in my sheets. Rolling onto my stomach, I ride my fingers. Energy burns through my body, and I ride the wave through its swell, and then, like a wave, I crash.

THREE

"**M**otherfucker!" I yell. "That better be some damn fine pussy." My heavy footsteps echo down the expansive hallway of my best friend's house. The storm of anger brewing in the pit of my gut intensifies with every stride. The volume of the moans increases as I grow closer. "I've been calling your phone for the last hour."

The door to his bedroom is open when I approach. I lean on the door frame and clear my throat to get his attention, my large body casting a shadow across the room. The asshole actually has the audacity to look up at me from between the legs of a busty blonde.

With a shit-eating grin plastered on his face, he says, "It is, Cass. You should have a taste." Then he places the woman's legs on his shoulders and drags his tongue through her wet pussy.

"Garrett," I roar, my voice bouncing off the walls.

Fuck my life right now.

I have Ruby's kiss of death hanging over my head and more pent-up energy than I can handle, and he offers this woman up like she's a Thanksgiving turkey. I need to fucking hit something, and if Garrett doesn't move his ass, it's going to be him.

The blonde looks up at me, her eyes hooded. "It's okay sugar, I've got room for two." Honey coats her Southern accent, thick and sweet.

"Garrett," I growl through gritted teeth. "Now."

He doesn't move from his position, only holds up a finger to give him a minute. If this were anyone else, he would already have a bullet between his eyes. But instead, I watch as seconds later the Southern belle on the bed writhes with pleasure and screams every name in the book except his. Laughter escapes me. I can't help it, even as angry as I am. Garrett uses the back of his hand to wipe his mouth and picks his boxers up off the floor. With one leg in, he stumbles toward me. I catch him by the arm, and he uses me to stabilize himself so he can get his other leg in.

He takes a deep breath and pats me on the arm. "Thanks, big guy."

I follow him downstairs to his office. Well, we call it an office, but it's more like a lair. There is no natural light, no windows. There's only one entrance, and Garrett and I are the only ones with access. He uses his thumb and forefinger to spread out one of his eyelids far enough for the retina scanner to do its thing. The door opens and a computerized British accent welcomes us. "Hello sir, I've been a bad girl."

"Got sick of *hello masterfucker*?" I raise an eyebrow at Garrett's back.

"Eh, the chick before the one upstairs kept telling me she was a bad girl, so I would punish her by refusing to let her come until I told her she could." He shrugs his shoulders. "Sometimes I would force her to come just so I could spank her after."

"What's it going to be next week." I give a high-pitched voice my best shot. "*Hi ya, sugar, let's rodeo?*"

"Or maybe, *Hey, y'all, let's go fishin' in the dark*," he quips. The fact that he came up with that one so fast makes me think he'd actually been thinking about it.

"What's the 911?" he asks. His fingers hover over his keyboard, preparing for battle. Computer screens cover every inch of the wall behind him. Video feeds roll on some, and code appears and disappears on the rest. The video feeds are the only thing of interest to me, the bar staff is breaking down the bar for the night, the parking lot is nearly empty. The code is complete nonsense to me, but it's Garrett's language.

"Ruby." I groan, my voice is gruff with indignation and laced with embarrassment.

"Fuck." His breath hitches. "When?"

"A few hours ago."

"And you're just telling me now?"

"Well, if you had picked up your fucking phone an hour ago, you would have known." I slam my palms on his desk. The alarms going off had fucking done it for me. I need to find this bitch now.

Garrett looks at me, eyebrows raised. "Why not a few hours ago when it fucking happened, jackass?"

"Why didn't you pick up your fucking phone?"

"I was exploring the south, my dear sir," he says with a smirk.

It takes all my self-control to not pound the smirk off his face and go make the Southern belle scream my name. I've never once hit Garrett though, and he knows I never will. A friendship like ours is forged on broken homes and fucked up families. We are all we have. Even if I don't deserve him.

"You're supposed to be the best tech guy there is. You didn't spend all that time sneaking into college classes so that you could dedicate your life to hunting and eating pussy. Get your head out of your ass and find out how she got into my cameras at the bar. Then find out how the fuck she got into my alarm system at home. And I swear to fucking God, Garrett, if I don't have answers before that girl in there comes again, I will kill her while you watch."

His fingers are typing a mile a minute before I even finish my threat. He knows he's safe, but he can't say the same for her. I'm not one to hurt or kill without reason, but if she gets in the way of him doing his job, I will not hesitate. The Ruby situation is washing away my good guy camouflage.

"I want her real face and her real name. I want to know what she ate for breakfast and where she lays her head. Find out everything you can about her." I bark the orders at him and after a moment's pause, I add, "And I want to know exactly how her marks die."

"I'm on it, Cass."

I sink into the leather sofa and watch my friend work. His

fingers fly over the keys, the noise drowning out the sound of my blood pumping through my veins. Watching him in his element always amazes me, especially when I consider all we've been through. We spent our youth scamming people for food and clothes more often than I like to think about. We're both smart and calculating. Garrett's gift is tech, he can hack his way into anything. Honestly, if it's got wires, he can figure it out.

My kind of smarts is different. I read people. I can spot their tells and weaknesses. It's what makes us a good team. Which is exactly why I'm fucking kicking myself in the ass for not recognizing Ruby's con from the beginning. My eyes were on her the entire time she was in my office, how the fuck did she get the envelope on my desk without me seeing? She certainly played her part well, the bitch.

Garrett's face contorts, then slackens, and I know that face. It's the one he makes when he hits a wall. It never lasts this long though, and I can't bring myself to watch any longer. I lean back and try to get a little sleep, but the click-clacking of the keyboard keeps me awake.

"Cass," he murmurs after a few minutes, his tone suspicious.

I sit up, alarmed by what he isn't saying.

"She doesn't exist," he continues, cautiously.

"I assure you she does, her lips were wrapped around my dick."

"Do I want to know how she ended up on her knees?"

"Same shit, different day." I shrug. "Girl smiles at boy, boy dances with girl, girl sucks boy's dick."

"When are you going to listen to me, Cass?" Garrett asks

through clenched teeth.

I roll my eyes because he's being ridiculous and paranoid.

He stands to his full height and presses into my chest. "You realize that this is exactly what I was trying to prevent," he says pointedly.

He resumes his place at the keyboard. "Fucking idiot, Cass. All it takes is the right person," he pauses and gestures to the screens, "to infiltrate our inner fucking circle and everything we've worked so hard for falls right the fuck apart."

"Says the guy with the blonde belle in his bed."

"Seriously? Do you really think I didn't dig into every nook and cranny of that woman's life? Fuck, I probably know more about her than she does."

I drag my hands over my face, because he's right. I know he is. That woman would have never walked into this house if he didn't know every skeleton in her closet.

"Fuck!" My voice echoes in the enclosed space. My whole body feels tight, like my veins could pop like a fucking balloon. I'm almost afraid to move, but I need to hit something, for the anger to dissipate, so I can think straight. This isn't just my life, it's his too. It was my fault then, and it's my fault now. I'm such a fucking idiot.

"So, I get that yes, she physically exists." Garrett sighs like he's talking to a toddler. "What I'm saying is that as a person, she does not. She has no real name, no address, no photos. In fact, everything I'm not finding makes her a ghost. Nobody knows who she is, only what she does."

He brings up his findings on the large screen in the center of the wall. It's nothing but altered photos, question marks where faces should be. It's like a game of fucking Guess Who?

"It's the twenty-first century, how does a person not exist?"

As pissed as he is at me, his cheeks lift in elation. "She has a Garrett." He leans back in his chair and crosses his arms, clearly impressed with my nemesis' tech guy.

"Is her Garrett as good as my Garrett?" I ask him, not sharing his excitement.

He scoffs at me like I've just asked the world's stupidest question, and it's completely ludicrous that anyone could be as good or better than him. He replaces the not-Ruby photos with multiple new photos. Each photo contains a different face, and each face is accompanied by an obituary.

"Are these previous marks?" I ask. I recognize a few of them as players, but I can't seem to remember anything I heard about their deaths. They didn't owe me money, so I couldn't be bothered. Does one of their family members blame me for their deaths?

"Dude, how do you not know this?"

"I never really paid attention. I kind of figured she was just an urban legend. And let's be honest, I never thought that someone would be stupid enough to hire her to kill me."

"She didn't tell you anything? Not a single clue as to what she has on you?" Garrett asks, his brows creasing.

"What the fuck are you talking about?"

"That seems to be her thing—torturing people with information. Like, even if it's not the reason she was hired to kill them, she tortures them with their secrets. This guy here." He pulls a photo of a white man with balding brown hair to the forefront of the screen. "He was a teacher that was sleeping with a student, except nobody knew until after he died. His wife said she came home from work one day and there was a school uniform skirt on their bed. Another day she meets him at work for lunch and when they walk into his office there's photocopies of his affair covering every inch with a lipstick mark over the girl's face."

"So, she pulls pranks before she kills? Like a child? I thought this woman was supposed to be sophisticated?"

"She does and she is. It seems like she plays with her kills before she strikes, kind of like a cat does with a mouse. She wants them to know she's been there, wants them to know she could've already killed them. She wants her mouse to be scared and jumpy. Then she slits their throats and kisses them on the cheek."

"So that explains the letter, the kiss of death, the phone call, and then the alarms at my house tonight."

"Wait, she called you?"

"Yeah, to gloat about killing me. I told her I would kill her first, then hung up."

"Cass, you didn't?" He shakes his head in disbelief.

"I did. G, how'd she get into my network? How'd she get into both my home and my club networks?"

He takes a deep breath, clearly concerned but not surprised with my reaction to this entire mess.

"Her Garrett is good, but I'm better. She hacked you, and for that I apologize. I'll fix it so it can't happen again. But Cass, I suggest we leave them be."

"Just let them have access to my security systems? Are you out of your mind?"

"Listen man, this woman is a ghost. How are you going to find her and kill her before she kills you if you don't know a thing about her? I suggest we piggyback on her hack and track her movements in your system. That way, you'll know a little about what she's up to. You know she's got cameras that cover every inch of your house?"

Of course she fucking does. Which means I need to keep my poker face even at home.

Fucking hell.

Four

The early morning air is heavy with fog. It lingers over the expansive grounds, ominous in its own right. I walk quickly, my boots disappearing in the grounded clouds and reappearing every few steps when they dissipate. Shivering, I pull my sweater tighter around me. The barn sits about five hundred yards from the main house. You can't see it from the driveway, and it doesn't show up on the internet or GPS. It does not exist to the world, even as large as it is. From the outside, it looks like your stereotypical barn, right down to the peeling red paint in desperate need of repair. It even has white boards in the shape of an X on the large doors. At the smaller entry door on the right, I hold my wrist to the scanner. The red laser casts over my skin and beeps when it finds the chip, unlocking the door.

I enter the barn and walk along the path at the edge of the room, careful not to step onto the training floor with my outside shoes. It's empty, the room pristine, having not yet been touched this morning. Throwing knives glisten on a stand in the corner, a mannequin with more holes than a pin cushion stands opposite, and combat dummies fill one wall, waiting for their daily beating.

I follow the sound of voices up the stairs, past the dormitory wing and showers, to our meeting room. The murmurs quiet when I enter. It is not as much a meeting room as it is a sanctuary. This entire compound is a sanctuary. We're not a typical company, and therefore the meeting space is not typical. The room has been designed to be relaxing, full of lush pieces of furniture, warm soft throws, and an absurd number of pillows. Comforts that many of the girls and women who pass this threshold are not familiar with.

We are an army of misfits, and I am the queen of this kingdom. Like Legion, we are many. We exist everywhere and nowhere. Across the globe and back again. An empire ruled by queens and forged from death. Framed photos of my predecessors line the wall behind me. Someday my face will join them, and a new Ruby will take the throne, but for now I rule this Kingdom of Loyal Reds. It is not for the faint of heart, being queen. It takes a killer. And killing is what I do best.

Each kingdom serves a purpose, ours is to train the next generation of Reds. From here they are dispatched to other kingdoms, to serve under other Rubys. We recruit girls who come from similar backgrounds to our own. We are the abused, the broken, and the neglected. Our childhoods could haunt the devil himself. There are currently six recruits, girls ranging in age from six to fourteen. Occasionally we require their service prior to them becoming full-fledged Reds, but for the most part they only train until one of us retires or dies. Except for me.

My replacement must be chosen by me. And I have not yet selected. None of our recruits have skills comparable to my own yet. I was twelve when my predecessor named me as her successor. I could walk into a crowded room and slit a man's throat without anyone seeing a thing. Replacing me will be hard, and I make a mental note to start actively searching for a new Ruby. I can't live forever. Even the best die.

I take my place in the oversized chair in the front of the room. Instantly, I'm enveloped in the soft red velvet. The high back sits well above my head, a black iron crown adorning it. I used to love this throne. I would leave our meetings with a high that could only be rivaled by slaughtering a poor soul, but that high has been missing for months, replaced with unease.

Crossing her legs like a young girl, Rowan takes the seat next to me and presses a button on her tablet. An LED screen descends from the ceiling at the side of the room.

"Good morning, Loyal Reds," I begin. "Girls, your objective during this meeting, like in the last five meetings is to tie this ribbon," I raise the red satin in my hand, holding it out toward the young girls, "in a Red's hair without being caught. If you succeed, we will start our knife training. If you fail, we will continue our stealth and teamwork modules until you successfully pass this objective."

The youngest girl steps forward to retrieve the ribbon. Her steps are sure, her posture ready for battle. I offer her a smile, which she returns with a toothless grin of her own before resuming her position along the wall.

"Okay, let's begin. Unfortunately, we do not have a lot of time this morning as I have a high court meeting shortly." I am greeted with nods from around the room. There are nine Reds including myself in our Kingdom. We work well together, each with our own strengths. One of them has a medical degree, another designs our disguises. We all have a job here.

I gesture to Riley to begin as always.

She stands, bringing herself to her full height. Riley towers over most men, which draws attention. Because of this and her nurturing nature, she plays the role of housemother. She takes care of us. She keeps us fed, keeps us in clean clothes, and keeps the girls under her strict gaze. Her strength though is grifting. It is from her that the girls learn how to play their roles.

"The girls are making progress. Their table manners and social cues are in excellent shape, but we continue to work on body language and accents. We have been working on multiple things at once, and I think it's been a bit confusing for this group." She smiles warmly at the girls, and I am reminded why she is perfect for this role. The rest of us would have simply pushed them harder. "I would like to break it into one role at a time and see if we can master one before moving on to another. Is there one in particular you want them to start with?" She looks pointedly at me, waiting for my instruction.

I shift my gaze to the girls and try to remember their backgrounds. I know at least one of them has been sexually abused, and another, the eldest I think, survived the massacre of her family by playing dead. I have to tread carefully. So often our minds still require mending long after the physical wounds have healed.

"Let's go with Amelia." She's the one that saved me when I needed it most, maybe she will save one of them too.

Riley smiles appreciatively. "Girls, from now until further notice, you are all Amelia, a posh British girl who goes to an all-girls boarding school. Her family comes from old money. Da died when she was a wee babe, and Mum is a socialite. Everything you say, everything you do, every movement you make, must be as Amelia. Understood?"

"Yes, Miss," all six girls say in unison.

"Okay let us move on to our current marks. Reagan, could you please give us an update on Mr. Davis?" The girls take this as their cue to begin the work on their objective. They spread themselves around the room, a plan in motion.

Reagan stands, her dark hair pulled back into a tight ponytail. She's been a Red almost as long as Rowan and I have. She taps on her tablet and a man's face fills the screen.

"For those who weren't here last week, a quick background on Mr. Davis," she begins, her voice steady with years of practice. "Mr. Davis is a pro bono case. He is a white male, forty-one years of age. He's a divorced father of two. We received intel two weeks ago that Mr. Davis has a drug problem. Which in and of itself is not a big deal. It became a big deal when he started to take inappropriate photographs of his children in order to pay for his habit."

Normal women would react to this statement. Normal women would be visibly and audibly outraged. We are not normal women. If any of us feel the need to react to cases such as this one, we do so in private. We do not show weakness. Ever.

"And where are we in his timeline? Have you scheduled my services?" I ask, nudging Reagan along. While all of us are capable of taking out a mark, it is my responsibility as Ruby to perform such tasks, if only to keep the rumors alive.

"Per your instructions last meeting, we delivered the letter, and then we plastered his car with pictures of him in his underwear while he was at work. We also laced his wine with a laxative while he was on a date. The kiss print on the toilet paper in the bathroom was priceless."

Reagan updates the screen to show pictures, and collectively we show emotion. Laughter fills the room, and I can't help but think about what we would look like to an outsider. Maniacs I suppose.

She continues. "We delivered his kiss of death a few days ago. He is so far on edge that if we don't act soon, you won't get the chance to end his life before he takes matters into his own hands. I have scheduled your services for this week."

I nod, and we move on to the next mark. This one is a nurse who works with elderly patients. Photos fill the screen once again. We sit in silence as Reya explains the complexities of this case. We have been hired by a victim's son, who tried and failed to bring Ms. Whitlock to justice. Ms. Whitlock does not appear to be taking the threat of yours truly seriously. The abuse continues and, in many cases, appears to increase in intensity after we make my presence known. With her kiss of death being delivered last night, I don't want to run the risk of her hurting anyone else. I make the executive decision not to wait any longer. She dies tonight.

There is some shuffling and a scream ripples through the room. Rawlings has one of the older Amelia's faces down on the ground with the girl's wrists pinned to her lower back, the red ribbon clutched in her small fingers. Rawlings removes the ribbon from the girl's fingers and helps her up.

"You need to work on keeping your hands steady," she tells the girl standing in front of her. "Your hands were so shaky, it sounded like a fly buzzing in my ear."

Amelia huffs, pushing her shoulders back and her chin up. "Wait until my mum hears about this," she retorts, and then she turns her back to Rawlings and walks with purpose to her place along the wall.

"We got a new one this morning." Remy, the youngest of all the Reds, uses her tablet to bring a young man's face up on the screen. "This is Bentley Drake. We, I mean Rowan, hasn't really had time to dig yet, but we know he's currently a college student, and it looks like his hit may have been ordered by an ex-girlfriend."

The room nods collectively, as if we understand the dynamics that would bring a woman to this—hiring an assassin. But none of us know intimate relationships beyond the act of sex, so how could any of us actually understand?

"Okay, Rowan do what you do best and go digging for dirt on Mr. Drake," I say before turning back to Remy. "Rowan will share the information with us and then you and I will arrange a meeting to discuss where to go from there, yes?"

Remy nods in agreement, and then my case is the only one remaining.

Cassius.

I stand, and his gray eyes stare back at me from the large screen.

"This is an anonymous kill for hire. But honestly, even if it wasn't, I believe he would have made it onto our pro bono radar in due time. His name is Cassius Cross, he's twenty-eight years old, and he owns the club on 16th Street downtown."

"He runs the casino," Reya interrupts. "I recognize him from tracking other marks."

"Correct. Which makes him a tricky mark. He will not go down easily; he will fight back. Hard. Rowan has not dug too deep on Mr. Cross yet, but I have no doubt that he has a closet full of skeletons, including the kidnapping of a local girl and paralyzing her brother. I've got it under control for now but will call upon you if necessary."

I catch Rowan's eye, and she nods almost imperceptibly. I neglected to tell the group about the phone call and the alarms. Some things are better left unsaid. Some things are better left private.

With a wave of my hand, the meeting is dismissed. Rowan and I exit together, leaving the remaining Reds to mingle as they deem necessary.

"Do you plan on filling me in on what's going on in that Red head of yours?" She asks when we're out of earshot of the others. "Do I need to be concerned about you Rubes?" She nudges me with her shoulder and if it was anyone else, I might slice them from navel to nostril without a second thought. But Rowan is different, for a long time we were a team, inseparable even. As children, we were recruited around the same time, and she was my first friend, my only friend, until I became Ruby, and everything changed. But Rowan's never stopped trying and in a weird kind of way, she's still my friend, even if I don't know how to be hers.

"I'm not sure what you mean," I lie, not meeting her gaze, afraid she will see through my mask.

"Rubes, you're taking on too much. You have two hits in the next two days, and now you're taking on Cassius Cross on your own."

"You know that I'm capable of the hits. It's nothing that should worry you. And besides, Mr. Cross is proving to be interesting, and he threatened to kill me. I can't leave him to the devices of others. Have you made any progress finding the girl?"

We enter Rapunzel's tower, Isabella's face lights up every screen.

"She's haunting me," Rowan admits. "I can't find her. I see her in my dreams, only they aren't dreams, they're nightmares, and in them, he's hurting her."

"We'll find her, Rowan," I reassure her. "I will cut off pieces of him until he reveals her location. Meanwhile, get me a list of all his properties and all his associates. Can you also arrange to have his car replaced? I think we should force him to drive something a little better on gas, don't you?

FIVE

My glass vibrates where it sits on the table beside me. The bass from the bar upstairs can be felt, even if the music can't be heard. I spend most of my nights down here, at the micro-casino, if I can. I enjoy watching the people, reading them. It's my own kind of game, knowing my players. It's why I'm so good at running the games, well that and the fact that I know how to count cards, which makes spotting it that much easier.

Like the douchebag sitting across from one of my best players right now. He's fucking counting, and he's not even good at it. *Fucking idiot.* I sigh and drain my bourbon. My skin crawls with unspent rage. The audacity of this man to come into my fucking game and pull this shit is ridiculous.

The fact that he fucking sucks at it makes it even worse.

I nod to Nate, who catches my eye from the doorway. In two short strides, he has one of his massive paws on the small of the cocktail waitress' back and ushers her out of the room. No reason to scare her or put her in danger. I am a gentleman, after all. Adrenaline ripples through my body, and I stand. The room around me goes still, ice stops clinking, cards stop shuffling. The bass from the bar only intensifies my energy, as if it's egging me on.

I don't say a word. I don't need to. I can practically hear their heartbeats with every step. Every player I pass by inhales deeply. I never used to consider myself a scary man, but this world turns us all into people we never thought we'd be. People who maim, people who kill, people whose presence instills fear. People like me. People like Ruby. The thought of Ruby and her bullshit only fuels my anger.

I extend one leg out in a swift kick, knocking the tall chair out from underneath the fucking trash bag who sits on it. The hypocrisy of my anger is not lost on me, it never is. But don't fucking cheat a cheater. The man stumbles to his feet, towering over my six-foot frame by at least four inches. A smile spreads across my face; I fucking needed this. I shift to my toes, ready for a fight.

The man throws a punch and I dodge it. *Fucking hell, that's disappointing.* I land a kick to his chest, and once again he falls on his ass. Fuck this asshole and fuck this bullshit. I pause for dramatic effect, giving the rest of the players the chance to really see me in action, using it as a warning. I make a move toward him, deliberately stepping on his hand, feeling the bones crush beneath my foot. Agonizing screams echo through the silent room. In a practiced move, I remove the belt from my pants and maneuver myself behind the jackass. The leather wraps tightly around the man's neck, his pulse fighting against the restraint. The more his body twitches in response, the more mine ignites, until finally he stops breathing.

I remove my belt from his neck and replace it around my waist. Nate immediately retrieves the body from my feet to dispose of it. I didn't intend to kill him. I had only meant to make a point. Which, on inspection of the room, I did. The players nod at me, respect dripping from their foreheads. I smooth out my shirt, adjusting one cuff and then the other.

"You do not cheat Cassius Cross," I announce to the room, as if they need an explanation. My heart pounds in my chest, the adrenaline that failed to release during what I expected to be a fight aches to escape. I need to fuck. I need to fuck now. I dial Garrett on my way up the stairs.

He answers on the first ring. "Not dead yet?"

"That belle still up to play?"

"Ask her yourself," he says, and my phone switches to video call. I tap on the accept button and am immediately rewarded with a live feed of the blonde's bouncing tits. Her moans of pleasure light me on fire.

"I'll be there in five."

The camera angle adjusts as Garrett props it up, offering me a better visual.

Technology. It's a wonderful thing.

I exit the club through the back door, and enter the parking lot, looking up from my phone. My parking spot is empty. I spin around. What the actual fuck? I'm so confused,

I parked it here this morning. I walk closer. In the impala's place, illuminated by the security light above, is a painted set of lips. Motherfucker.

"Where the fuck is my car?" Waves of fury crash over me. The fucking bitch took my car.

"Garrett," I yell. "Where the fuck is my car?"

His face fills the screen for what feels like an entire minute before he answers me.

"It's in the lot."

"No, the fuck, it isn't." I spin around, showing him the employee lot. The Impala is nowhere to be found.

"Yes, it is, walk sixty feet to the left, GPS says it's right there."

I follow his instructions, my long strides making it there in only a handful of steps. The car in front of me however is not my fucking Impala. Instead, it's a fucking hybrid piece of shit with handicap plates. A set of red lips on the rear window. As I approach, the lights flash on the car and the doors unlock. Dark clouds hang over me, the weight of what I've done sits on my chest. Ruby knows, but how much does she know exactly?

"Garrett."

"Yeah, Cass?"

"The girl. Is she safe?" My voice hardens with each word.

"The girl? Safe?" Garrett questions me, his voice lifting an octave.

"The fucking girl," I bellow, my hands forming a fist at my side. "Is she fucking safe, Garrett?"

"Oh, that girl, yeah man. Nobody will find her."

I release the breath I was holding. A small penance for

my doubt.

"Change of plans," I tell him. "I'm not in the mood to share tonight. I'll find my own pussy. And Garrett?"

"Yeah, man?"

"Find my fucking car."

I hang up the phone and stare at the ugly ass hybrid sedan. It seems I have two options, either I can drive away in this ridiculous thing and likely crash because the whore cut the brake lines, or I can call the car company I utilize in the winter when the Impala goes into hibernation. Neither feels right though. Ruby has proven to be smart and calculating. It's her job. So, she would have anticipated those options and would have prepared for me to make either choice. The right choice appears to be not to make a choice at all.

But I know people too, and thanks to Garrett, I know Ruby has a signature. She wouldn't blow up the car or cut the brake lines. No, she wants to slit my throat. If I call the car service, it won't be here for at least fifteen minutes. If I drive the hybrid, I can have my cock between a set of pouty lips in under that.

The driver's seat feels foreign to me, the pedals at my feet are all wrong, and there's no place to insert a key. Instead, there's a button that says *engine on/off*. Using my middle finger, I push it, and immediately the dash and control panels illuminate. The engine is barely audible. If it weren't for the lights, I probably wouldn't have been able to tell the fucking thing had even started.

The display screen for the radio goes black for a second, and when it turns back on, Ruby is looking at me. Her deep brown hair falls in loose curls around her face, and I can't help but picture those curls splayed across my sheets. My gaze shifts to her lips. Pouty. Red. Lips.

Fuck me. Get it fucking together Cross.

"Good evening, Cassius," she purrs. Her tongue caresses her bottom lip before taking it in her teeth.

This bitch. My teeth clench and my knuckles turn white on the steering wheel. My interactions with her so far have been brief, but Ruby's presence is electrifying. There's something about her that claws at me, threatening to undo everything I've worked so hard for. Awakening emotions I suppressed long ago and breathing life back into me. Gone is the numbness I've felt for so long, and in its place is this electric current running in my veins.

"Let's play a game, shall we?" Ruby asks with an impish grin because we both know it's not actually a question. We're going to play a game whether I want to or not.

"Does it involve your lips on my cock again?" I flash a smile at her, hoping for a reaction, but her face is still and unamused. Just the thought of her on her knees again has my dick pressed against my zipper, begging to be released.

In response, the gear shift on the car shifts into reverse on its own. I try to push it back into park, but the effort is futile, and the car begins to back out of the parking spot.

"What the fuck are you doing?" I roar at the screen. I pull on the door handle, but nothing happens. I try to unlock the doors, but again nothing happens. In a last-ditch attempt, I try the windows, but it's with wasted effort.

"I have control of your new motor vehicle, Cassius, is that not obvious?"

"This is how you're going to kill me? Seriously?" I can't

help but roll my eyes at her. "I think I deserve better, don't you?"

The car pulls out of the club's lot and onto the busy downtown street.

Ruby's brown eyes narrow, her lips pull tight, "Where. Is. The. Girl?" She says each word with punctuation, applying pressure to her question.

"I've been with a lot of girls; you're going to have to be more specific," I retort, a smirk playing across my face.

The car jumps the curb onto the sidewalk, and my body tenses involuntarily. The time on the dashboard says it's late, almost last call. I need to get us out of downtown before the clubs close and the sidewalks are full of pedestrians. I may maim and kill without mercy, but I don't do it without a reason. Innocent people don't need to die because this bitch has a vendetta against me. I put my arm behind my head and lean back into the seat. If we're going to be at this for a while, I might as well make myself comfortable.

"The girl Cassius. Where is the girl?" Her eyebrows furrow, her bottom jaw tenses. Her frustration with me is growing and it's hot as fuck.

"Do you have a name? A picture? A picture could jog my memory, maybe. I might need a picture of her ass though, in case I fucked her from behind, in which case I probably wouldn't recognize her face."

"The girl you stuffed in the trunk of your car, where is she?" If Ruby could shoot lasers out of her eyes, I'm pretty sure they would be aimed at my face right now.

The fact that she knows about this is proof that Garrett was right, she has a tech guy, or girl, digging and they're good.

Because I'm guilty of exactly what she said. I shoved a terrified young girl into the trunk of my car. And I don't regret it for a single second.

I bite my lip, deep in thought. Okay not really, but I need to gain distance, away from innocent people. When the car navigates back down the curb and takes the next turn down a side street, I speak again.

"I don't have any idea what you're talking about, a girl in the trunk of my car?" Tapping my finger to my chin, I repeat, "A girl, what girl?"

The car immediately jumps the curb again and crashes through a wire fence, beelining toward a rundown house. The pounding in my heart increases in speed, matching the throbbing need in my dick, but I don't flinch. She won't kill me. Especially if she's looking for the girl. Ten feet from the house, the car reroutes, sending dirt and grass flying into the air.

The release I'm so desperate for, the one I neglected to get earlier, is bubbling to the point of overflow. And I don't know what's pulsing harder now, my heart or my dick.

"I'm sorry, baby, I don't know who you're looking for." I'm a glutton for punishment and I know it. I want her riled up. I want her frustrated and confused so she can't stay away. I want to bury myself inside of her while she negotiates with the grim reaper to take me down.

The speedometer on the car nudges past fifty, and the increase in speed only feeds my inner adrenaline junkie. The wheel cuts to the left, lifting the passenger side tires off the ground. Brick scrapes the mirrors on both sides as the car cuts through an alley, causing sparks to fly in the dark night.

The noise drowns out the sound of my zipper.

"You know Cassius," she begins. "I really do need some new garland for my Christmas tree. Your intestines would do quite nicely." Her eyes light up like the very Christmas tree she speaks of, one corner of her mouth lifting in a sly grin.

I fist my cock. If she notices, her poker face is as good as my own.

"Face it, sweetheart, you don't have a Christmas tree. You would need a soul for that."

Uncomfortable silence fills the air. I struck a chord; apparently soulless Ruby has a weakness. My laughter breaks through the emptiness and the car pummels through a park, coming within mere feet of a tree and then veering away. She's playing a game of chicken with nature...and my life.

My cock is like stone in my hand, almost so hard it hurts. My grip tightens and I slide my callused hand up to my tip, pre-cum coating my fingers. On the screen, her red lips are pursed in a displeasing frown, and I want nothing more than to smear that lipstick, make a mess of this woman. See her come undone.

"The girl, Cassius. Where is she?" Ruby holds a picture up on the screen and my heart plummets a little. The picture has been photoshopped to show a healthy teenage girl. But she wasn't. Not when I took her.

"You'll never find her," I bark through gritted teeth. "You don't even know her fucking name."

"Isabella Diaz, and I assure you I will find her," Ruby retorts. The car pulls out of the park and onto the road, narrowly missing an oncoming car.

"I repeat, where is she?" she demands, and my climax

JESS ALLEN

grows closer.

"You have no idea what the fuck you are talking about, you crazy fucking bitch." I imagine the fight that would ensue upon my words if we were in person and not speaking through a screen. The adrenaline pushes through me as I slide my hand up and down my shaft. Rock fucking hard and raw from friction, but I can't stop. I need this release more than anything I've ever needed before.

The car increases speed. Sixty, sixty-five, seventy. I pump faster. Seventy-five now. We weave in and out of cars. I sit somewhere on the brink of death, and yet I feel more alive than I have in years. Fucking monster, that's me.

"Cassius." My name rolls out of her perfect mouth, each syllable breathier than the last.

A guttural moan escapes me, and my eyes seek hers, desperate for her to say it again. Silently pleading with her. I need to hear it dance along her tongue and spill from her lips, deadly like a poison without an antidote. Because it could kill me, and I'd die a happy man.

I don't actually know if she can see me, but if there's a God, I pray to Him that she can. I shift in the driver's seat, angling myself closer to the screen, like she could reach through it to touch me.

"Cassius." Her breath hitches and her lips purse when she swallows.

"Ruby." I growl her name as my cock opens fire at the display, coating a digital Ruby in my cum. I run my palm over my length, coating it with my own seed to soothe the burn and I shudder, I don't know the last time I came so hard. Every nerve in my body is charged. Closing my eyes, I try to terminate the live wires and savor the moment.

When I open my eyes again, the display is dark. She's beginning to live up to the rumors. Maybe she is a ghost.

Horns blaze around me, cars swerve out of the way. The car hits the rumble strip, and I take the wheel. I'm now in control. Of the car. Of Ruby. Of whatever game we are fucking playing.

I hope.

Six

"Rubes?" Rowan's voice echoes in the attic.

My eyes meet hers.

"Did that..." I start.

"Yeah," she mutters. "It did."

"Did he know that we could see him?"

"I think so."

"It's like he sees me," I admit more to myself than to Rowan.

Rowan gives me a pointed look and I stand from the chair, knocking it over in the process. It's not like me to get flustered. It's not like me to let things get out of hand like that. Ruby does not act this way. Ruby does not allow herself to be treated like this. Ruby is a ruthless killer. Ruby is emotionless.

I am Ruby and therefore I am numb. I do not feel. Feelings make you weak, and Rubys are not weak.

I am Ruby.

I am numb.

I do not feel.

I am not weak.

I'm Amelia, and I'm twelve-years-old, playing a part while Ruby tells me I am to be her successor. She doesn't smile when she says it. She doesn't offer congratulations. Instead, she attacks my mind. Abusing it, day after day, until I learn to be like her—void of life. She tells me it makes it easier to take others. That it's for my own good. Ruby is merciless in my training; it's far worse than any other recruit's. The other girls are allowed to smile and cry in their therapy sessions. Not me. I'm supposed to talk about my parents' neglect without emotion, like a robot.

At night in the dormitory, the other girls talk about falling in love when they retire from the Reds. They dream of their futures, of the women they will be, of the person they will spend forever with. But not me. I'm not allowed. The only relationships I will ever have are with the recruits I share a room with. I don't know what it means to be loved. My parents didn't love me. Ruby doesn't love me. Nobody will ever love me because Rubys are queens and queens don't retire.

They die.

Rowan sees the single tear that slides down my face before I can wipe it away. She offers me a forced smile but doesn't say anything. There's nothing she can say, sometimes life just happens to you. And when it does, you can either let it mow you down or you can transform yourself. I did the latter.

"I need more Row," I tell her.

She looks at me, her eyebrows pinched, as if she is not sure what I am talking about.

"More skeletons," I explain. "Cassius has not reacted like any other mark thus far. In fact, it seems that the more I try to get from him, the harder I push him, the more infuriating he gets. I need dirt so that I can put a rush on his timeline."

Cassius is cracking my foundation with every interaction, exploiting the weak spot Rowan unearthed last night. And if he can crack my foundation over the airwaves, what could he accomplish in person?

"I need to go," I start.

"Change your panties?" Rowan asks, her eyes glinting with devious thoughts.

"Kill a mark. And Row? This did not happen, okay?"

She nods her head and repeats, "It did not happen."

My face narrows. Shooting her a glare, I leave the attic. Fuck Cassius Cross. Irritation bubbles beneath my skin. Killing this man is going to be one of the greatest pleasures of my life. The arrogant prick will meet my blade soon. I will not wait to find the girl. My trust in Rowan runs deeper than my loyalty to my name. She will find her. We will bring her home.

S even-two-four-six. My gloved fingers press the numbers on the keypad and the deadbolt slides out of place. The knob turns easily and without a sound. I open the door and cross the threshold. Years of training keep my steps light. Silent. Moonlight filters through the kitchen windows, offering a small sliver of light in the dark house. I follow the hallway with the moon at my back. Counting each step like I have in the weeks prior; I get to fourteen and rotate ninety degrees to my left. Practice makes perfect. Tonight, the moon is my friend, but we don't rely on friends or lights. Lights draw attention, but people tend to ignore the things that go bump in the night. They blame it on animals or say it's the house settling. Darkness is our home. It's where the Reds thrive and grow.

The door is open, like it has been every night I've visited. Routines can be dangerous. My heart does a little flip inside my chest as I enter the room. My pulse quickens with each step. Six, seven. I retrieve my blade from its sheath in my boot. I leave the rope at my waist, intent on a fight and climb into the bed. The mark stirs at the shift in the mattress but doesn't wake. I rest my head on the pillow beside hers. Do all divorced women still sleep on one side of the bed, or is she an anomaly? Does her bed feel empty without another body to keep it warm?

Does mine? Surely not, but I've never known otherwise.

The air has changed, absent of shallow breath. I turn to face my mark.

If fear had a taste, it would be sweet like candy. Lucky for me, I have a sweet tooth.

"Shh," I coo into the darkness.

"P-please," she stutters.

The mattress shifts beneath me as the mark retreats to the edge of the bed. I let her. She climbs out of the bed quickly, but I'm quicker. The alarm clock on the nightstand offers enough light that I can see her outline. I grab her by the hair. Wrapping it around my hand, I drag her back onto the bed. She claws at me, drawing blood.

Fucking bitch.

I stab one of her hands with my free one. A scream of agony escapes her, and it's a concerto to my ears, only accompanied by the fast beating of her heart. I stab at her other hand. Whimpers fill the darkness, joining the orchestra. Straddling her, I press my knees into her injured hands and release her hair.

I lean in close, my face inches from hers. "Did they beg too, Ms. Whitelock? Did they say please? Did they cry out in pain when you hit them? When you starved them? When you let them sit in their own excrement? Did you enjoy playing God? Did you enjoy the pain suffered from your hands? Was it worth it?"

"It wasn't me," she whispers.

"I enjoy the pain I cause," I answer. "But devils do not play God." I use the blade of my knife to caress her cheek. "You are going to die, Ms. Whitelock, but I am curious why you did it?"

"To...to," she stammers. "Fill the silence."

I'm swift with my blade. It slices across the tender flesh of her throat. Blood sprays back at me while her heart continues to pump. Showered in her blood, Cassius plagues my thoughts like a virus that can't be contained. Cassius knows what I do, he knows his death is imminent, and yet he called out my name. In the throes of his own pleasure, no less.

This game we're playing. It's not cat and mouse. It's not predator vs. prey. I know this game, and I know that the queen is the most powerful. She does not live by rules. She hunts and kills without remorse. This is a game of strategy, and I have a lifetime of experience.

Chess is the first thing recruits are taught when they come to us. We use it to teach how to focus on more than one thing at once, and to think multiple steps ahead before we make our move. I bombed that lesson at first, but before I trained to be Ruby, Rowan and I were paired together on most tasks even though she was two years older than me. And Rowan, she was incredibly intelligent, even as a child she was smarter than most of the adult Reds, although they would never have admitted it. She helped me understand the game, and I helped her survive blade training. Together we were unstoppable, but like chess, time eventually runs out and when it does, someone has to lose. For a long time, I thought it was Rowan, but I'm starting to think it was me. That becoming Ruby wasn't the prize I thought it was.

Blood and water blend together as they swirl down the drain at my feet. Scrubbing my skin, I finish washing away Ms. Whitelock. Her blood and her memory. When I leave this shower, I will not think of her again. We all do what we must to forget, make amends and lock the memories away. In my shower, I wash away the sins of my legacy.

But her last words eat at me because I cannot make sense of them. To fill the silence? What the hell does that mean?

Was it their screams? Their cries for help? Or did she mean the emptiness? The one that creeps up on me between jobs. Where my thoughts and feelings bounce around in a deep cavern with nothing to brace their impact because that's what my training required. And when I kill, it feels as though the cavern is suddenly full of every thought and feeling, and they hold on to each other, leaving no space for air. Maybe it's the same thing, silence and emptiness, and maybe me and Mrs. Whitelock are more alike than I thought.

I'm toweling off when a video call comes through on my tablet.

"What did you find?" I answer, not bothering with hello.

"Okay, so Mr. Cross," Rowan starts. "He one hundred percent committed a hit-and-run on the girl's brother. The teen is paralyzed from the waist down. Honestly, he's lucky to be alive."

"How do we know for sure?"

"Incoming video."

I press play and watch as Cassius' Impala slams into a teenage boy crossing the street. The driver climbs out—his build instantly recognizable as Cassius. He walks toward the boy, leans in to check his pulse, then climbs back in the car and speeds off.

"And the girl?"

"We have a transaction report from his credit card company. He purchased clothing from a women's boutique downtown and heavy chains and locks from the hardware store. And Rubes?"

"What else Rowan?"

"Incoming video."

Fucking Christ. I knew it was true. My sources are never wrong, but I really wanted...to be honest, I don't know what I really wanted. For it to be lies? For him to be a better person than me?

I tap my finger on the play button and hold my breath.

Cassius walks down the street, dragging Isabella Diaz at his side until he pushes her into the trunk of the Impala. The video is not the best quality, but as someone who can taste fear, I feel like I have a cavity. The young girl is terrified. I freeze the frame. She looks a lot smaller than the photo we have.

My improper thoughts of Cassius should be forgotten after seeing this. He's a monster. But so am I. And what is it that people say? Like attracts like? The realization hits like an earthquake to my cracked foundation. Bricks of the walls that hold me together, that make me who I am, begin to fall.

Forcing the queen to make her move.

SEVEN

It's taken a few days to find her, but there she is sitting at an outdoor table, her light purple hair glistening in the afternoon sun. It's short, cropped at her chin with straight bangs and large sunglasses sit on her small nose. The disguise is impressive. And I'm thrown by how gorgeous she is. Even like this, even when she's someone else. She's deadly and captivating, and I hate her. I hate her for being the thing I crave most. The present I want to unwrap, layer by layer, until all I see is her. Who is she behind the disguises? Behind the blood and the violence? Is she full of demons too?

A waiter approaches her, but Ruby doesn't turn to look at him. Her gaze appears to be focused elsewhere. With those large sunglasses, it's hard to determine exactly what she's looking at, but I'm willing to bet it's a target. Her lips move, and she raises her hand, effectively dismissing the waiter.

She's fascinating and the more I watch her, the more captivated I am. Everything she does is intentional; every slight movement is calculated. A routine. One she's done over and over for the last fifteen minutes. First, she looks at her phone and scrolls for a moment, then she pulls her lips to the left, always to the left as she turns her head in both directions. Looking for someone who isn't coming, I'm sure. After she does that she crosses and then uncrosses her legs, flashing her red bottom heels and takes a sip of her drink. Then the routine starts again.

Cars pass in front of me, obscuring my view for seconds at a time. When traffic slows, she's gliding her finger in circles around the rim of her water glass, like she's bored. That's new. She doesn't get lost in her phone again either, but instead pulls a paperback out of her tote bag. To anyone else, it would appear that she's reading, but she hasn't turned a single page. Her focus lies elsewhere. Maybe on the couple a few tables away? The man is young, much younger than the woman he's dining with. Is it her? Or Him?

They're arguing, quiet enough that none of the other patrons pay attention, but her eyebrows narrow, and she speaks through gritted teeth like she's doing that whisper yell thing I've seen moms do. Is she his mother? From here, she looks old enough for it to be possible. His lips move and then his head tilts. His cheeks lift in a smile...and nope. Not his mother. That's not the kind of smile you give your mother. That's the kind of smile you flash when you want to get laid.

The woman flushes and places a pile of cash on the

table. The couple stands to leave, picking up the handful of shopping bags at their feet. Chanel and Tiffany's for her. Gucci and Burberry for him. Is it her money or his?

It doesn't matter because Ruby is stone faced now, a lioness preparing to pounce. She throws a handful of bills on the table but doesn't move from her seat.

I stand to get a better view over the traffic.

The woman walks past her first, the man's hand guiding her forward. Ruby doesn't move, guess the woman must not be the mark then. They take one more step, Ruby flicks her wrist, and her glass of water practically throws itself at the man.

She stands, her hand raised to her mouth in shock as the man yells. Ruby grabs the cloth napkin off her table with one hand and holds it out to him apologetically. If I had any doubt that it was her, it dissipates when her other hand slips a red envelope into the Gucci bag.

The couple exits the café through the small gate and continues down the sidewalk. Ruby watches them, a wicked grin spreading across her face. She grabs her tote bag and walks inside the café. I take a deep breath, that smile is going to plant itself in my nightmares and awaken my demons. And when it does, I hope hers are ready to play.

Garrett is the only reason I knew where to find her. I'm not lying when I say he's a motherfucking genius. He created an algorithm that snapped pictures of every Impala in the area from traffic cameras and private security cameras. Then he took those and cross-referenced them with Ruby-like events, and that landed me here, stalking an assassin.

I wait for her to exit through the door and onto the

street. But I lack patience, I'm an instant gratification kind of man. My skin crawls with anticipation. Afraid that I've lost her, I don't walk to the crosswalk. Instead, I wait for a break in traffic, so I can cross. The door to the café opens, and I halt at the curb, frozen. A woman exits. It's not the woman I expected, but it is the same tote bag. Her purple hair has been replaced with a sleek blonde ponytail. One I'd like to wrap around my fist. The sunglasses are gone, replaced by rectangular eyeglasses that frame her small face. She walks quickly down the street, and I force myself to wait until she is a block away before I cross. I don't have her chameleon abilities, but I'm hoping, like Joe, my baseball cap will be enough.

The city street is soon crowded with suits on their lunch break. Luckily, being six feet tall has its advantages. I spot the blonde ponytail a few yards ahead of me but keep my distance. She walks quickly, weaving between strangers oblivious to the devil in their midst, and it urges me forward. I have never been one for hunting, again I lack patience, but there's something about hunting Ruby that has me craving a trophy. Albeit not one that hangs on the wall, but maybe one strapped to my bed.

She walks slowly past a window display and then seemingly changes her mind, backpedaling a few steps to the entrance. Tucking myself into a food truck line, I stay out of sight. The door chimes as she enters, the sign above it reads Davis Appliance Repair.

I call Garrett.

"Yo," he answers. "How was the intel?"

"You know it was good. Tell me about Davis Appliance

Repair," I demand. "And quickly."

The tapping of keys on the other end of the line fills the silence.

"Bankrupt. Owner is divorced. Nothing too outlandish, but let me run my Ruby tracker on him."

More tapping.

"What's your plan?" Garrett asks me.

"Plan?"

"Yeah, you do have a plan, don't you? To kill her?"

"Don't have one yet, but I figure I can always just shoot her."

"That's not like you."

"It gets the job done." I sigh. "Anything on this Davis guy yet?"

"Yeah, he'll be dead soon if he's not already. Dude took pictures of his kids. Someone tried to scrub them, but I will bleach the shit out of the dark web."

I hang up and free myself from the crowd, following in Ruby's footsteps. The door is locked, and the open sign has been turned to closed. I could break the glass and stop this, but I won't. This man deserves what's coming to him. Cupping my hands to block the sun's glare, I peer through the window. Ruby is nowhere to be seen. There are shelves full of parts and a vacant sales counter. It's empty. Eerily empty. And much quieter than one would expect. It's certainly quieter than when I kill someone. Past the sales counter, there's a door that must be a back entrance or emergency exit. I take off, weaving through the handful of people on the sidewalk and turn down the narrow side alley only to come face to face with...

Ruby.

Black ringlets frame her face, bare now of glasses. Her eyes tinted dark with makeup. This was not part of the fucking plan. Not that I had one, but that's beside the point. I only planned to watch. To observe. But now she's in front of me close enough to touch and fuck me, I want to touch her. I need to touch her. There's something about her that sings to me like a siren's song. Tortured and beautiful.

Her eyes widen for a second and a sinister smile creeps over her face.

Come out to play little demons...

"Cassius." My name drips like honey from her lips.

"Ruby," I say, flashing her the smile that's worked on a hundred women before her. I take a step forward, but she doesn't retreat. She's used to being the alpha. The queen. She opens her mouth to speak, but no words come out because my hand has her by the throat, pushing her against the brick building. Her teeth bite into her bottom lip, her long lashes hood her eyes. I am not falling for this, nope. I should fucking kill her right now and be done with it. No more chasing, no more games. I reach for my gun in the back waistband of my jeans and press the cold steel to her forehead. She sucks in a breath, her tits lifting just slightly. And fucking hell if she doesn't smell like vanilla with a lingering tinge of iron. An overwhelming need to taste her passes over me.

Just a taste.

Putting the gun back in my waistband, I push my body against hers, my hard length pressed between us.

"You smell like death," I whisper, my lips grazing her ear.

"Your favorite, I presume," she croaks out.

I pull back to see her face and remove my hand from her throat. She remains still, her eyes penetrating mine. She cocks her head, curiosity falling over her features.

"Why did you call out my name?" she asks softly. She looks so confused and so innocent that it takes me a few seconds to collect myself.

I place my hands on the wall on either side of her, and her breath quickens.

"I knew you'd enjoy it," I answer, and watch as a blush creeps into her cheeks. "Tell me Ruby. Did you touch yourself after?"

"Do not flatter yourself."

"You wanted to. Just like you want me to touch you now."

Her sharp intake of breath is her only tell and had I not been inches from her lips, I would have never heard it.

Game fucking on.

EIGHT

Cassius flips his baseball hat around and a soft moan escapes my lips. I can't help it. Full and hungry, he presses his lips to my own. I allow his tongue entry, but he only teases, pulling away to taste my lips again. He does this over and over, until I can't help but want to touch him. I reach for him, desperate to feel him beneath my fingers, to glide them over his body, but his hands encircle my wrists, bringing them above my head.

"You may be the queen, but this," he hisses, "is my fucking kingdom. You are not in charge here."

My breath hitches, on the verge of explosion, and all he's done is kiss me. I need more. I arch my back, silently pleading with him.

With one hand holding my wrists, he uses the other to lift the skirt of my dress. His fingers trail lightly over my panties, teasing with a breath-like touch. He slides my panties to one side and slides one finger between my folds, navigating to my clit before retreating again.

"Tell me what you want, Ruby."

The answer should be a simple one, but it is not. It is a trick question because the things I want most are things I can't have.

All I can do is nod.

Cassius pulls his hand out from between my legs, his eyes clouded with lust.

He licks the pad of his thumb and swipes at a spot beneath my eye. He holds it in front of my face, so I can see the spot of blood that coats it.

"You missed a spot," he says at the same time his hand returns to my panties.

He doesn't waste any more time teasing me. He applies light pressure with his thumb and then flicks softly. When I let out a barely audible moan, he rubs harder. His fingers glide through my wetness as he works my clit. His eyes hold mine, and he pushes a finger inside me.

Then two, working them in and out of me. I have to close my eyes and I try to catch my breath, but the feeling is so intense that I feel as if I will burst.

Twisting my body, I fight against his hand holding my wrists. The restraint is almost too much, the need to touch him, to run my fingers through his hair, to scratch at him, to feel his length in my hands. It eats at me. I open my eyes, he smiles, a dimple popping up on one side, and a shiver runs through me. Fuck, he's a masterpiece. A picture-perfect specimen sent from the devil himself to torture me. He increases the pressure on my clit and my legs start to shake. I squirm, trying to pull away, but too easily he reads my motives. His body presses against mine, trapping his hand between my legs.

"Let go, Ruby. I got you." He abandons my pussy, his focus solely on my clit, and I moan appreciatively.

His lips form a knowing smile as he increases the intensity. This time I will not hold back. My legs shake, and I lose the strength to stand. My breath catches in my throat. The orgasm that rips through me overflows. It spills over my edges; it splashes down my legs.

Cassius pulls his hand from beneath my skirt and takes a step back, looking down at the small puddle on the pavement. He licks his lips and releases me. Using both hands, he rubs at the red areas on my wrists, raw from his grip.

Then he lifts his hands above my head and jerks them to one side, his eyes pulled together in concentration.

"What are you doing?" I ask.

"Fixing your crown." He flashes a smile. "It was a little crooked."

He flips his hat back around and retreats out of the alley. I lean back on the wall, my feet no longer able to move. His strides are long and sure, and too soon he disappears around the corner.

I got what I wanted. Right? So why do I feel like a queen who just had her kingdom invaded?

Because I acted impulsively, that's why. From the moment I let him track me, I played him. I made the moves

I wanted to. I let him see me, follow me. I made a point to be visible. I locked the door at the appliance repair store so he would wait. I hadn't expected him to corner me in the alley. I hadn't expected my back against a wall, my juices dripping from his fingers. But he read me like a fucking book and left me craving more.

Worse, the smug bastard knows it. My fingers twitch for my blade, desperate to spill more blood. A safer alternative.

Safer for my heart, at least.

NINE

A guttural, "Yeah?" comes through the speaker of my phone.

"Where's my fucking car, Garrett?"

"Lot on Thurston Ave. It's white."

I hang up. The fucking cunt painted my car. I walk quickly, needing distance from Ruby. Composure is the only thing I have left, and I will not lose it in front of her. Two blocks later, I sink into the seats of my Impala. She may have painted it since the last time I saw it, but the interior hasn't changed one bit. The leather still holds my impressions in its memory. The same way I hope Ruby's pussy does.

I press my foot down on the clutch and turn my spare key in the ignition. The engine roars to life. Part of me wants to roar with it, the adrenaline rushing through me like a high I've never felt. I got close to the beast, so close I felt her juices dripping from my fingers, fuck she even splashed my fucking shoes, and I am still here. I survived to tell the tale.

I peel out of the downtown lot and onto the street, swerving in and out of traffic until the city buildings look miniature in the rearview mirror. The lingering scent of vanilla hangs in the surrounding air, strong and sweet. I pull down a country lane, empty except for the fallen autumn leaves.

Shifting gears, I push the speedometer higher, a single thought plaguing me. Why was that so easy? She's a chameleon, a grifter, a woman of the shadows. A woman who's never been caught. So how the fuck was Garrett able to find her so easily? And why was I able to trail her in the light of day?

Because she fucking planned it. *Motherfucker.* She wanted it. She wanted me. She still wants me. She really is the damn queen, and fuck me if that doesn't turn me on more. Ruby only submitted because she herself wanted to. She let herself fall apart at my touch, literally. She could have killed me right there and honestly; I probably would have died a happy man with her tight pussy clenched around my fingers.

"Fuck!" I yell to the empty car, my voice carrying on the wind through the open window.

I pull the emergency brake and turn the wheel, spinning the car back in the other direction. A horn blares, and I swerve, barely avoiding a semi. Throwing my head back, I let out a maniacal laugh, and then dial Garrett.

"She wants me," I tell him when he answers, but I don't

let him respond. "You said she has cameras all over my house, right? That Southern belle down to put on a show?"

Thirty minutes later I punch the numbers at my gate while Belle, whose real name is Cadence, considers my proposal. Contrary to popular belief, I am a gentleman so it's very important to me that she understands exactly what she's getting into, even if she doesn't know the real reasons behind it.

"If you don't want to do this, you don't have to, but I need to know now. I want to remind you that I don't know who will be watching the feed, and I don't know if it will be recorded."

She bites her full bottom lip before nodding her head. "And if the video ever gets brought up in a way that hurts me or my reputation, Garrett will make it disappear?"

"Yes."

Her cheeks lift in a sly smile. "And in return, you'll get my sister and her kids away from her abusive husband?"

I nod. I don't tell her that I would have done it without her help. Maybe that's the difference between me and the gentleman I claim I am.

"Let's go make a movie."

Thank fucking god.

TEN

Rock music blares from the speaker on my dresser. I carelessly flip through the clothes that hang on the bar in my closet—finding nothing. The fabrics are wrong. The patterns are wrong. The cuts are wrong. Everything is fucking wrong, and I can't tell if the music is calming me or putting me more on edge. It's a fine line. An alarm rings on my phone, it's incessant wailing clearly audible over the music. It takes a moment for it to register with my brain, but it's the motion alarm for Cassius' home. I quickly mute the music. Curiosity eats at me. If I haven't stopped thinking about our earlier interaction, does that mean he's thinking about it too?

I grab the remote and flip the large television in my suite to channel Cassius. The cameras filter through until they find motion. Cassius stands with his back to me at the kitchen counter, his body language unreadable. But then he drops to his knees, revealing a woman sitting on the counter with her dress hiked up to her waist. And oh, my Lord. He is not. Oh shit, he is. I press the power button. *Breathe Ruby.* But I can't. My breath hitches in my throat. Warmth spreads between my legs, and I do exactly what I shouldn't.

I turn the television back on.

I know better than this. I am better than this. But sometimes the need to rebel simply overpowers my resolve and once I start, it's difficult to stop. My body feels like a pipe under pressure. And pressure needs to be released or things burst.

His lips trail down one of the woman's legs and then the other. Attentively. Seductively. Savoring every taste. Shivers run up my body like it's me he's worshiping. He pushes her legs to the side one at a time and then buries his face between them. Her eyes close and her mouth opens, ecstasy written all over her face. I turn on the volume, a glutton for punishment. Small whimpers pass through her lips when Cassius moves a hand from her knee to between her legs. My thighs clench, remembering the alley. Her hands rake through his short brown hair and her moans get louder until finally her legs quake. But Cassius doesn't let up. He maintains rhythm until her body once again relaxes.

I should call Rowan. She'll be my voice of reason. And I start to. I really do.

But then Cassius lifts the woman from the counter, her legs wrapped around his waist, and they leave the frame. I fill my lungs and exhale with disappointment. Again, the cameras filter through until they find one with motion. He has the woman bent over the arm of the couch, her ass in the air. He unbuttons his shirt, one button at a time, and then removes it. I fall into the chaise lounge and pull the knot on my silk robe, committing myself to something I'm not sure I can come back from.

Cassius slides one hand between the woman's thighs, and the other works on removing his belt. I press the button that brings up all the camera feeds and find that this particular place can be seen from multiple angles. I bring them all up on the screen. Cassius rips a condom open with his teeth and slides it over his impressive cock while he finger fucks the woman on the couch. With an open palm, he lands a slap on one of her ass cheeks, and she yelps with surprise. That same hand grabs the woman's blonde ponytail while he uses the other to guide himself inside her.

With her ponytail wrapped tightly around his hand, he pulls. And I can't take it anymore. I slide my finger between my slick folds and work my clit, increasing the intensity every time Cassius increases his speed. He is ferocious. A beast that cannot be tamed. He pulls her head back and pinches her nipple until she screams. My fingers are no longer doing the work I need them to, and I growl in frustration. I retrieve my vibrator from my bedside table. Caressing it with lube, I fall back on the chaise once more. I slide it between my legs and adjust the settings. The clit stimulator pulses slowly and then increases in strength before dropping speed again. I rock the vibrator in and out of myself until it grazes my g-spot.

A growl escapes Cassius' lips and my floodgates open like he commanded it. Like he speaks my body's language. The thought, equally terrifying as it is tempting.

He spanks her ass. He's not done. I'm not done. I'm begging him to spank me too. I'm writhing in my own pleasure and simultaneously jealous that I'm not the one bent over in front of him.

"Fuck yes, you're so deep," the woman cries, and I want to cry with her. Every semblance of self-control is gone.

"You're so fucking wet, you dirty slut," Cassius says. "You love my cock, don't you?"

"I want to taste it."

My mouth waters at the thought of having Cassius' dick inside my mouth again. The silky head at the back of my throat. His balls in my hand.

"Maybe next time, you..." He says as he angles himself deeper. "Naughty. Girl," he growls, punctuating each word with a punishing thrust.

Once again, the woman's legs shake until Cassius and the couch are the only things holding her up. He removes himself and picks her up. Then he throws her over his shoulder like she's nothing more than a doll. Weightless.

The cameras toggle.

My vibrator stalls. Where did they go?

A whimper leaves my lips. Pipe. Must. Burst.

The cameras once again find them, this time in the bedroom. Give me more Cassius. I need more.

Even if it breaks me.

ELEVEN

Tossing Belle onto my bed, I bury my face between her breasts and kiss my way up her sternum, along her collar bone until finally reaching her ear.

"You good?" I whisper, praying I'm only audible to her. She pinches my thigh twice, a signal we worked out in the car that means she's okay, and we can keep going. I roll us over, and she lifts up on to her knees, sinking down on my dick. She works her hips back and forth, rolling them in circles, trying to find a rhythm. This is her show now. I let her find her own pleasure. When she finally does, she rides me like a fucking bull. Like the true Southern belle she is. Rough and without remorse. I tease her clit with my fingers, and she bucks harder and faster, chasing her own release.

I flip us again, pulling one leg over my shoulder. I move her own hand to work her clit while I pound into her. Skin slapping skin, the muscles in my ass clench with each thrust. I pull a nipple in between my teeth and give it a tug. She whimpers, and I release it.

"Come for me, baby," I whisper. "Come for me, Ruby." It's a command.

Her legs tighten, her toes curl, and her face contorts into one of pain and pleasure until finally her entire body relaxes, and she peers up at me through hooded eyes.

I remove myself from her clenches and remove the condom from my still hard dick. She's not Ruby. I need Ruby. My dick needs Ruby. I go to the bathroom and turn on the shower, letting it warm before I get in. I wash Cadence's scent off me, wishing it were a metallic vanilla instead. My balls ache, but I don't relieve myself, preferring the punishment.

I close my eyes, a lifetime of indiscretions flooding me. The rich fucks I cheated as a teen. The girl caught in the middle, dead on my doorstep. The blood. Garrett's screams. My silence. It all comes back, fresh as the day it happened. Years of blackmail, torture, and death. The sound of Isabella's scream as I pushed her in my trunk. The fear in her eyes when I opened it again.

Fucking masochist. That's what I am. Reliving the shit that haunts me day in and day out. I roll my shoulders and turn my back to the water. The heat from the water eases the tension in my body, and I start to relax.

When I get out of the shower, Cadence is no longer in my bed. I get dressed quickly and find her sitting on my kitchen counter, clothed, eating an apple.

She shrugs when she sees me. "Sorry sugar, I was hungry."

I raise my hands in a no problem gesture. "You ready to go?" I ask. She nods in answer, and I grab her hips, lifting her off the counter. Gentleman, see?

In the safety of the car, under the cover of the moon, we're quiet. The only sound to be heard is the car purring beneath us.

"Back to Garrett's then?" I ask.

Cadence sighs, doing so with her whole chest, like she's been waiting for me to ask but didn't want to break the silence herself.

"Nah, I think I'm gonna go home." She pauses for effect or because she's still deciding, I can't tell. "Yeah, I'm gonna go home and pack."

I tilt my head in her direction, leaving the question unspoken between us.

"I'm gonna go with her, my sister. I think she's gonna need me."

I don't tell her, because I don't think she's the kind of girl who needs validation for her actions, but I think she's doing the right thing. Her sister will need all the support she can get, especially in a town where she'll have no one.

"You got it, sugar," I say, trying to imitate her accent. She laughs and other than Ruby coming, I think it's the sweetest sound I've heard in a really long time.

We drive the rest of the way in companionable silence. Sometimes people need the quiet. Sometimes the quiet helps us heal. It's in this moment, sitting in a car with a woman who quite literally just sold her body to save her sister, that I finally decide I don't want to live a lie anymore. I want to be able to forgive myself, and I can't without others forgiveness first.

Twenty minutes later, I pull up to a small apartment complex, and Cadence turns to look at me. She leans in, brushing a soft kiss on my cheek. "Call me if you need me again," she says softly, and then climbs out of the car, closing the door behind her.

"Cadence, if you ever need anything, you get a hold of G. Got it?" I tell her through the open window.

She nods and gives a small wave before walking up a set of stairs. She walks to her apartment door and unlocks it to let herself in. The door closes behind her, and I pull out of the lot.

I drive through the city and out the other side. Past the outskirts and into the mountains. The car glides around the curves, like I imagine my hands gliding over Ruby's. Slow and with purpose. I pull into a scenic view pullover on the side of the mountain and turn off the engine.

And then I wait. I wait beneath the stars for Ruby to find me.

TWELVE

I lean into the curve of the road; my body feels like it's only inches from the pavement. I shift my weight coming out of it and increase my speed. The motorcycle growls beneath me and I push it even faster. There are no cars on the road, but at two o'clock in the morning I didn't expect there to be.

My heart thunders in my chest. Pounding with thrill and fear. Excitement and worry. It's a feeling I relish in. One I don't think I've ever felt. I'm not scared of Cassius. I'm not worried that he'll harm me. But I am scared of how I feel around him. I'm wavering. Teetering precariously close to the edge. One I'm not sure I can back away from.

His car sits at the scenic pull in. Ominous beneath the moon. The white paint reflects in my one headlight. He lies on the hood of his car, his hands beneath his head. He doesn't move when I pull my bike up next to him.

I kill the engine. The night is quiet. Still. The city below us is so far removed from where we are that it's like we're sitting on a cloud. My movements are silent, and even though he knows I'm here, he startles when I lay next to him.

"You requested my presence?"

"You came," he says matter-of-factly, as if I'm not sitting next to him. He turns his head to look at me, a smug smile creeping across his face. "But did you come, Ruby?"

Fuck this arrogant prick. Forget every thought and feeling that has penetrated my armor. In one quick movement, I'm straddling him. Blood trickles down his cheek where the tip of my blade presses into his skin.

His eyes close, and he inhales deeply. Curious. So curious. I can feel him growing hard beneath me. Removing myself from this situation would be in my best interest. It would be. But I don't move. I don't dare move. If I move, it will be to grind my pussy over his length. I will not move. I can't move. Moving would be a mistake, for both of us.

"Your scent is intoxicating, Ruby, the perfect mix of vanilla and blood," he says, his words carrying on the empty air.

I tilt my head, really taking him in. How is he so relaxed? His arms still folded beneath his head, his body hard with muscles and wanting, but completely calm and still.

"You are intoxicating, Ruby. Has anyone ever told you that?" His features are muddied in the dark, but his eyes twinkle in the night sky. They look into mine, but I don't look away. If I do, he wins. And I don't lose. Ever. "You are sexy as fuck after you kill someone and fuck me if the thought of you killing me right here, right now, doesn't have my dick standing at fucking attention."

"Is it me?" My breath hitches. "Or is it fear?"

"Both."

I glide my blade across his jawline, not drawing blood but showing him I could. It barely grazes his skin, enough to get my point across. He removes his hands from behind his head and places them on my hips. I pull up, trying to distance myself from his hard-on, but he pulls me back down and grinds me back and forth across his erection.

My blade twitches in my hand, and I press it into his neck, once again drawing blood. He does not stop though, he just drags me harder along his length. I slice into his chest, my dagger easily cutting through his shirt to his skin. Blood blooms on the fabric. Still, he doesn't stop. He takes one hand and puts it on my throat. His fingers dig into my neck, and I can't breathe. Not because he's choking me, but because I'm so close to coming for him for a third time today.

Every time I hurt him; he pushes me harder.

I need it to … to … I need it to stop.

I spin the black steel of my dagger around my finger, the rubies on the hilt glimmer in the moonlight. Spinning it into position, I control my grip and plunge the shallow blade into his stomach. His hold on my throat tightens, and he uses his massive size to flip me to my back.

"Fucking bitch," he growls as he lets go of me.

"Fucking prick," I retort.

"I need to be inside you."

"You need to die."

Cassius climbs off me, removing his shirt, and uses it to apply pressure to his wound. It's not fatal, but I needed to interrupt whatever the fuck was happening between us.

"Who says?"

"I do not reveal my clients, Cassius. That would only put a price on their head, and then we would be stuck in a never-ending loop where I would run out of people to kill. And Cassius—I really like to kill." I say the last part through gritted teeth. "I need to kill." I admit.

"I like when you kill, baby. Just not me."

I turn towards him, eyeing him warily. He called me baby and fuck; I actually liked it.

"What if I double your fee to not kill me?" he asks, his voice flat.

"I do not break contracts."

"But if you kill me, you won't be able to fuck me. And we both know you want to."

My phone dings, and I pull it out to look at the screen.

Rowan: Where are you?

I look at the time, I have not been gone long. What could she possibly need?

On assignment.

Rowan: Why is your location turned off?

Must be a glitch.

Rowan: Or a dick. Get home before someone else notices you're gone.

I climb off the car, my heart no longer thundering in anticipation. Its beats are slow and rhythmic. Back to normal, I suppose. Cassius extends an arm out ... to stop me? To pull me back? I don't know, but his injury is substantial enough to put me outside his reach. I will always be just outside his reach, and he will always be just outside of mine. True intimacy will always be a pipe dream.

I wish it was one I could chase.

I hold the clutch and push the start button on my bike. The motorcycle roars to life. Part of me wishes I could do the same.

A cloud of dirt is all I leave behind.

Thirteen

"So, you gonna tell me what happened last week or what?" Garrett asks me, reaching for his glass on the table. We're sitting in my VIP booth at the bar. It sits a few feet above and to the right of the DJ booth, providing a fantastic view of the dance floor and bar.

Flashes of color illuminate the bodies on the dance floor. People of all shapes and ethnicities move to the music. The DJ has them fired up, their skin glistening with sweat beneath the lights.

The bartenders are hustling, throwing bottles in the air and catching them with ease. Cocktail servers deliver drinks with a soft touch for a customer here, a caress there. The tips they will pull in tonight alone will cover their rent for the month, if not two. The different games in progress downstairs stay visible via the tablet on the table in front of me.

I slowly lean back into the soft booth, careful not to tear my stitches, and take in Garrett sitting a few feet away from me.

"You remember when we were kids, and we would ride our bikes in that neighborhood with the flowers?"

"You mean the bikes we stole?"

I can't help but laugh. "Yes, those bikes. Do you remember the neighborhood?"

"The one with the um…" He huffs. "What the fuck were those flowers called, they were purple, right?"

"Yeah, but the flowers aren't the point. You remember the neighborhood?"

"We used to pop those suckers." Garrett smiles, his own train of thought not yet on course with mine.

"Fucking hostas G." I glare at him. "Again, not the point. Anyway, you know how there was that huge ass hill, and we would ride down it with our eyes closed?"

"Those were the fucking days, Cass. Man, I miss that shit."

"And sometimes," I continue, "we would take our hands off the handlebars? Scared shitless that we would crash, but also seeking the high of it?"

"Yeah, man."

"That feeling? I haven't felt that way in a long time. Even when I'm torturing some poor sap that got in over his head. Or killing that guy the other night? It was just work. Same shit, different day. And the worst part is, I didn't even realize that's what was missing until her." I signal to the bar for a refill and finish the drink I've been babysitting for the last half hour in three sips. "Because Ruby? She's like an active bomb, and I just want to be the one to cut the right wire, but I'm also feeding off the fact that she could blow."

Garrett's head tilts to the side, his brows furrowed. "Can't you just go skydiving or swim with sharks like a normal person?"

"Only you would think that shit was normal."

He shrugs his shoulders. We both know he craves that shit too. It's why he's constantly getting his dick wet. In his case though, it's about the one who got away. The one he couldn't have, and the one he couldn't save. He won't admit it, but I see through him. He looks for her everywhere, but she's gone, and she can never come back. You don't come back from death, but it doesn't stop her ghost from haunting him. Hannah's been haunting him since we were sixteen years old.

I think a part of him will always blame himself. He watches the crowd grinding on the dance floor, a smile plastered on his face, but it's just a prop. It doesn't reach his eyes. It never does.

That tired old story, the one about the girl from the suburbs falling for the guy on the wrong side of the tracks? That shit was Garrett's real life until it was his very real nightmare. Her dad forbade Hannah from seeing Garrett. He took her car so she couldn't go to him, but that brave ass girl got herself on the bus. It would be her first and last time. Her broken, bloodied body waited for us on the front porch of my house. Garrett and I were both arrested for her rape and murder but were eventually released when a video of us shoplifting at a local store confirmed our alibi. If we had gotten home sooner, maybe she would still be alive. If she and Garrett had never met, maybe she would still be alive. If I had made a different choice, maybe she wouldn't haunt us both.

Garrett's eyes widen slightly, the only tell that something is off. I follow his gaze and see two detectives flanking my empty-handed waitress. Their worn, ill-fitting suit jackets giving them away. Not only is she bringing cops to my fucking table, but she's doing it empty-handed. I make a mental note to fire her after I get rid of the pigs.

The detective to her right sees me and slows. He's an older guy, with graying hair and a little weight around his middle. He puts out an arm in front of the waitress to stop her and turns to say something in her ear. Her momentum slows and then stops. She glances up at me, and I nod her my permission. She scurries back to the bar.

The other guy is a rookie, but it's not only his young face that gives it away. It's his bravado. The guy has no idea that he walked into the wolf's den. The moment he sees me, his chest puffs and his movements quicken. I bet he creams his pants before he even gets his dick out. In his mind, he's big and bad. In everyone else's, he's earnest and asking for a fight he cannot win.

He's the first to arrive at the booth, his eyebrows stand at attention over his dark eyes, and he widens his stance in an attempt to look larger. Garrett and I make eye contact across the table, rolling our eyes in tandem. Is this guy for real?

"Cassius Cross?" he asks, his voice barely audible over the music.

I tap an index finger to my ear and lean forward, my face screwed up in confusion.

92

"Cassius Cross," he says louder this time.

I strain my head closer, pulling my large body out of the booth just enough that the rookie takes a startled step back.

"Cassius Cross," he screams this time.

"Jesus Christ," the seasoned detective yells, finally joining the circus. "He's sitting right fucking there."

He gives the rookie a pointed look that reads, *shut your damn trap.*

A laugh escapes me, and I nod my head in greeting to the two men.

"Cassius Cross," the rookie begins, and the older one actually slaps him upside the head.

"Collins, shut the fuck up and let me do my job." The older detective pulls a badge out of his coat pocket, and the rookie follows suit. "I'm Detective Larson and this is my idiot partner, Detective Collins. Mr. Cross, could you come with us down to the station? There's a matter we would like to discuss."

"There's a matter you'd like to discuss. At midnight?" I scoff, my eyes narrowed.

"Mr. Cross, we really would prefer to not make a scene, so if you could just come with us," Larson pleads, his voice weary with years of long hours. Collins shifts his weight side to side, his anticipation palpable.

"What's this regarding?" Garrett asks, and both men look at him as though they only now notice he's there.

Larson sighs. "It's a private matter."

I slide my body out of the booth, if only to see Collins shit himself. I stand, my tall frame towering over both detectives.

"C-Cassius Cross," Larson stammers. "Turn around and put your hands behind your back. You are under arrest for the kidnapping of Isabella Diaz."

"I will not," I say. "You said you didn't want to cause a scene. Don't cause one. I'll come with you, no cuffs."

Larson grazes his eyes up and down, sizing me up. "I don't think so, Mr. Cross. Just turn around and let's be done with this."

Collins fidgets beside Larson, his hand ready on his gun. If he pulls that out, it's going to be chaos. Innocent people will die from mass hysteria, so I concede. When I turn around, Garrett has already pulled his laptop out of his bag and his fingers are tapping at the keys, working his magic. He doesn't look up once, not even when Larson slaps the cuffs on my wrists.

"You have the right to remain silent..."

Fucking Ruby.

FOURTEEN

The young girl throws a bag out of a first-floor window. The homeowners remain undisturbed, the house dark. She climbs out after the bag, her feet landing softly on the ground.

She closes the window silently and disappears into the night. I stay close, like I have all evening, moving as her shadow. She can't be more than ten, yet she controls her slender limbs with the grace of a dancer. She's not clumsy or awkward like most prepubescent girls.

She moves with confidence, sticking to the darkness beyond the streetlights.

After hitting the eighth house, she takes to the woods with only the moon to guide her way. I slow my steps, increasing the distance between us. The woods make it harder to be silent. She climbs over downed trees and ducks under branches with such ease that my heart flips in my chest. Her abilities rival my own, and she is only a girl. We only need to hone her skills and teach her the language of the blade until she's fluent.

The girl reaches the train tracks and turns to follow them north into the city. She walks on the rail like a tightrope. A voice carries over the night air, and the girl stills. As do I. We have a visitor. A second voice echoes with the first. A bottle sails out of the woods and makes contact with the tracks in front of the girl, shattering at her feet. She takes a step back, then another, her foot slipping. She steadies herself. It's the first time she's faltered. I remain at the edge of the woods. Observing. The decisions she makes in the next moments will determine her fate.

She crouches, placing the bag behind the railroad tie, hiding it from view. Whatever's in that bag, she doesn't want our visitors to find it. She tucks her blond braid up into her beanie and pulls up her hood. She has nowhere to hide, so she can only hide the fact that she's a girl and hope they leave her alone. Smart, but will it be enough? The boisterous duo rambles forward, emerging from the woods.

The moment they see her, time seems to stop. They take the child in, and then look at each other before turning to her once more. Their carefree demeanor shifts to that of a predator. They move purposefully, as if they've done this before. One of them clears their throat and spits, walking around the girl, removing her escape route.

"It's a little late for you to be wanderin' these woods

alone, ain't it, kid?" the spitter asks, his voice that of a career smoker. It grinds in my ears.

The other man wipes his nose with the back of his hand and chuckles, clearly the lackey. The girl must sense this, because she turns, coming face to face with the true threat.

Spitter leers at her, taking his bottom lip between his teeth. The realization that he doesn't care whether the child is a boy or a girl hits me the same time it hits her. She takes a step back, but Chuckles is there to push her forward into Spitter who backs up. She stumbles forward and her hood falls. Her blond hair peeks out beneath her hat.

She stands tall, as tall as a ten-year-old girl can. The grown ass men stare down at her like she's dessert, but no tears fall. She doesn't cry. She doesn't yell out. She lunges.

"Motherfucking brat," Spitter yells, outrage pouring into each syllable. "She fucking stabbed me."

Chuckles grabs her from behind, lifting her off the ground. A shard of bloodied glass is visible in the moonlight as she brings it down into Chuckles' upper thigh. He releases her, but Spitter is ready for her.

I don't wait a moment longer. I emerge from the shadows and jump on Spitter's back; my blade slicing clean through his carotid. Warm blood coats my hand, splattering in front of us. The girl uses her free hand to wipe blood out of her eyes, stunned either at the amount of blood or the sight of me, I'm not sure which. Chuckles moves for me, but I land a kick to his chest, knocking him to the ground. I straddle him, and in seconds, I am showered with his blood.

"Do you have a family?" I ask the girl.

She removes her beanie and uses it to wipe the blood

from the rest of her face. Her small shoulders lift in a shrug.

I repeat myself, "Do you have a family?"

She shakes her head. "Not one that matters." Her voice is small, but her confidence is so big that I am taken aback once again by her age.

"What's your name?"

"Alice."

"Well, Alice, my name is Ruby. Let me formally welcome you to the Loyal Reds."

R owan spins in her chair and claps like a sugar-crazed child.

"Told you, Rubes."

"Rowan, she's perfect. You should have seen her tonight. She might end up being a better Ruby than me one day."

Rowan scoffs and moves back to her keyboard. Cassius fills multiple screens. He sits at a table in an interrogation room with his arms crossed over his large chest and a vein pulsing in his neck. A uniformed officer stands sentry in the corner, waiting for Cassius to make a move.

"Has he cracked at all?" I ask.

"Nope," Rowan replies, popping out the p.

She presses a button, and we hear a detective ask, "Is she dead, Cassius?"

Cassius rolls his neck and stares at the camera.

The detective speaks again, "Where is Isabella Diaz?"

Cassius does not break eye contact with the camera, when he asks, "Where is the supposed video?"

We hear paper shuffling off-screen, but the detective doesn't answer him. A knock sounds, and the scratching of the chair sliding on the floor follows. A door opens and closes. Cassius continues to make eye contact with the camera. With me. My skin prickles under his gaze.

The door to the tower opens, and I nearly jump out of my skin. Reagan enters. Rowan quickly changes the programming, but I'm not sure if she was fast enough,

"Ruby. Rowan," Reagan greets us, her tone peculiar. She looks pointedly at me. "I just wanted to let you know that Alice is settled in. You might want to let her be for a day or two before you begin training. I have a feeling she's been through quite a bit. She has some serious scarring on her legs and sides."

My heart plummets for the young girl, but I know she's safe now.

Reagan smooths her ponytail out of habit, not necessity, and offers a small smile. She did not need to come up here to tell me this, and yet here she is. What does she really want? She turns to leave and then changes her mind, turning back to us once more.

A fake smile creeps over her face. "Oh, Ruby, I was also curious where you were in the timeline for Cassius Cross? Isn't his time up?"

I grit my teeth, anger, and embarrassment swirling together inside my body, both trying to reach the surface. "We haven't found the girl yet."

"Oh, but I mean, we don't actually need him to find her,

do we?"

Rowan remains quiet beside me. She's not a fan of the others invading her space.

"Actually, Reagan, it would make things so much easier if we are able to force him into complacency."

She nods her head, and sucks on her teeth. Rowan and I exchange a knowing glance. Reagan is clearly not convinced, but she doesn't question us further. When the door clicks closed behind her, I hold my hand up to Rowan, stopping her before she starts. We're not going to have this conversation, because there's nothing to discuss. What we told Reagan was all true. We haven't found the girl yet, and it really would be easier with Cassius alive to tell us. That's all.

I offer Rowan a forced smile and make my way out of the attic, my normally sure footsteps leaving a trail of uncertainty in their wake.

FIFTEEN

I f fury were a color, it would be deep red, almost black.
Toeing that line that you can't come back from. I see it,
the red, black seeping into the edges. I'm going to kill her.
And I'm going to enjoy it.

Detective Larson sits across from me, leaning back in his
chair, arms splayed wide.

I have no idea what he just said. I don't care what he said.
I'm going to kill her.

More words come out of Detective Larson's mouth, but
I'm not listening.

I'm planning her murder.

It's only when he reaches out to shake my hand that I
piece together the words. Sorry. Confusion. Free to go.

I don't shake his hand. I'm a man on a mission.

I exit the precinct into the early morning light, using my hand to shield my eyes. After five hours of sitting under the dim and flickering lights in the interrogation room, the sunlight is blinding. Garrett pulls up beside me in his truck, and I climb in. He starts to say something, but one look at me changes his mind.

We drive back to the bar in silence. When we finally pull into the lot and I climb out, I can only manage a "Good work, G" to show my best friend my appreciation.

It's all I have in me.

He nods in understanding.

The cleaning crew for the bar starts at 8 a.m. which gives me only a couple of hours to be alone before they start showing up. I let myself in and lock the door behind me before climbing the stairs to my office. I slow when I reach the landing, sunlight filtering into the hall through my office window, the door ajar.

Cautiously, with the stealth of a fucking gorilla, which is to say no stealth at all, I step over the threshold. Ruby sits back in my chair, her red bottomed heels propped on my desk. She spins a small black dagger on my desk, the blade digging into the wood, similar I think to how she pictures killing me. I close the door behind me and stand there, my feet sprouting roots. She stops the dagger mid-spin, lifting it into the air a moment before I hear the whistling beside my ear. The dagger clangs when it hits the metal door, hurling itself out of reach. I reach up to touch my ear, my fingers coming away wet and sticky with blood. She kicks off her heels, and they fall to the floor with a soft thud.

The world turns from deep red to midnight black.

Fire burns within me, prickling my skin and propelling me forward. My body slams into hers before she can react. The chair rolls across the floor, and we crash into the wall, a mess of limbs and splintered wood. Drywall dust clouds my vision long enough for Ruby to slip from my grasp. She circles behind me and kicks the back of my knee, forcing me to the ground. The move is practiced and swiftly delivered.

Cold steel presses against my neck. Her warm breath grazes my ear.

"Look at you on your knees," she purrs. "You wish it were me." It's a statement, not a question, and I would be lying if I said she was wrong.

"You fucking cunt," I say through gritted teeth, and I ram my fist backwards to meet her nose.

Pain pierces my neck, but only for a split second. The heat of Ruby disappears, and I stand, turning around to face her. She wipes her face with the back of her hand, blood smearing across her menacing smile. Her tongue swipes across her lips. Memories of her licking my cum off them rush through me.

I push the thoughts down, burying them in the dark recesses of my mind. I stare at her, gauging my situation.

"Tsk-tsk." She shakes her finger, scolding me in a way that only a teacher at a boarding school could. Something plummets into my right thigh, and for a moment I am dazed, completely enamored by her skill at misdirection. When I look down, a throwing knife sticks out of my leg—black with a circle at the hilt and a red gem gleaming at the end.

"What else are you hiding up that skirt?" I challenge her,

pulling the dagger from my leg. It hurts like a motherfucker, but I don't let it show. I spin the dagger around my finger. Soon my walls will be painted red with blood. Only one of us will leave this room alive.

Practiced fingers walk up her leg, lifting her skirt up to reveal the garter, three more daggers within its grasp. I take a step toward her, slow and deliberate, committed to a game I'm not sure I can win. She's a statue. Not even her breathing disturbs her stillness. Another step, another dagger, this one grazes my arm, but I don't shift my gaze from hers.

One down, two more to go.

"I'm going to kill you slowly, I think," I tell her. "Take my time with you. Watch your blood as it spills from your veins and turns black on this floor."

Another step.

Another dagger. This one misses completely. This is progress.

"I'll probably have my way with you first. Pound that pussy of yours into submission." I tell myself that I'm only playing the game, but she takes a small, uneasy step backwards. I wonder if anyone has ever challenged her the way I have. If anyone but me has ever made her stumble before.

"Your hands tied to the radiator over there, my fist in your hair."

Another step.

Another dagger soars. It goes wide. The air in the room shifts.

An assassin of her stature, I doubt she ever misses.

Her hand flies to her mouth. Big brown eyes stare at me for a moment too long. A moment I use to close the distance between us. A bare foot kicks out at my chest, but I'm ready for it. My hand wraps around it hard enough to leave bruises if she lives. I yank hard.

The queen falls.

Her back hits the floor, dark hair spilling out around her. Her tits rise and fall with each breath she takes, her nipples hard, pressing against the thin fabric of her shirt. A surprised cry leaves her mouth, still red with blood.

My eyes roam her body, and I drink her in, like the top shelf liquor she is. When I make my way back up to her face, her hungry eyes stare into mine.

She uses one foot to kick into my thigh, right where her dagger speared me. I wobble, but don't fall. She swipes at my other leg, and I crash next to her with a thud.

She pulls herself to her feet quickly, putting space between us once again.

"You fucking bitch," I growl.

"Did you really think you could keep me down? The fucking queen who feeds off shit stains like you?"

I force myself up to my feet and cross the room to her in three strides. Her hands search her thigh for another dagger, but they're gone. I push her against the wall, my hand around her throat, sliding her up until we're face to face. Her legs kick at me, and her hands claw at my arms.

I really want them to claw down my fucking back.

I press closer to her, and her assault on me stills. She inhales sharply, stealing my breath from inside my chest.

My lips brush against hers when I speak again. "So, tell me, Queen, how's it feel to be bested? Do you still want to kill me? Or should I tie you to the radiator now?"

Strong bare legs wrap around my waist, effectively holding her up. I loosen my grip on her throat, and her tongue slides between my lips. I swallow her kiss. It's all consuming and soul crushing. I start to pull away, but her teeth sink into my lower lip, pulling me back in. My cock hardens, reveling in the sting. The taste of copper passes between us.

Her tongue dances across mine, forceful and angry. My hard dick rubs against her, and she bites my lip harder. Her nails dig into the graze on my arm, the pain causing me to let go of her. She tries to wriggle her body away from me, but she's snug between me and the wall.

She pushes at my chest and then throws a punch at my face. I dodge it, taking a few steps back. Her feet hit the floor with a soft thud. Grabbing one of her hands, I twist her around until her back is flat against my chest.

Releasing her hand, I wrap one arm around her shoulders to keep her still.

I trail my lips down her neck, and she shudders against me. My free hand explores her body, palming her breasts and sliding over her stomach, a heat seeking missile on track to find that sweet spot.

"You wet for me, Ruby?" I ask her, taking her earlobe between my teeth.

My fingers find their way beneath her skirt, a surprise waiting for me.

"No panties today?" A sharp intake of breath is the only response I get.

I slide a finger between her folds and am awarded with another whimper.

I don't prime her. That single finger is the only warning

she gets before I thrust two fingers inside her clenched pussy. Her body sinks into me. Releasing her shoulders, I palm her tits, her ass grinding against my cock. My fingers drive in and out of her, hard and fast, and she rides them with fervor.

I don't let up as I shift us closer to my desk. It's only when I bend her over it that my fingers leave her warmth.

"Don't fucking move," I snarl. I push her skirt up over her ass. Her perfect fucking ass that I can't help but spank. I use one hand to undo my pants and the other to leave my mark. She tries to roll to her back, but I press my palm between her shoulder blades, pushing her back down.

"I said, don't fucking move." Taking a step back, I admire the picture before me, my beautiful surrendering queen. I grip my cock, tempted to make her lay there while I pleasure myself, if only to coat her in my cum.

"You're so fucking beautiful when you surrender," I tell her through gritted teeth as I stroke myself. Her back arches, lifting her hips just so, silently begging me to bury myself deep. It seems I'm not the only one who can't help myself. Digging my fingers into her hips, I shove my cock into her waiting cunt in a single thrust. Fuck me. She feels as good and as tight as I imagined she would.

My head drops back in ecstasy, "Fuck, Ruby."

I am not gentle as I pound into her, my balls slapping at her clit with each thrust. Our chorus of moans fill the room, sticky like the blood that coats us. Reaching forward, I grab her wig, tugging hard. I need to know what beauty hides beneath the disguise. Nails dig at my hand, and I let go, wrapping an arm around her waist to hold her up. She fiddles around her hairline for a minute, then pulls off the wig, flinging it across the room.

Ruby red hair spills over her shoulders, rendering me still.

She places her palms flat on my desk and turns her face back to me, "Now pull," she commands.

I don't hesitate. I wrap her red hair around my fist and pull. Her back arches as I pummel her pussy. Her hands reach out, gripping the other edge of my desk. She cries out in pleasure; her ass tightens and her tight pussy clenches around me. Fuck. Me.

"Not yet, baby," I tell her, "I want to see your face when you come on my cock for the first time."

Need to see her face.

I pull out of her and flip her over. She pushes me back and climbs down from the desk. She fists my cock with a vise like grip.

Her hand on my dick guides me to the couch. "Sit the fuck down," she orders.

And I do, because she's the queen, and I'm one orgasm away from worshiping her on her fucking throne.

SIXTEEN

Cassius pulls his shirt over his head and throws it across the room.

This man.

He feels... so much better than my vibrator.

My hand glides easily up and down his shaft, still wet with my arousal. He relaxes on the leather couch, his eyes never leaving mine. Large hands grip my ass and pull me onto his lap. I release my grip and instead use my hand to guide him to my entrance. The silky head of his cock breaks the barrier, and I drive my body down. His hands drift to my hips, but I slap them away, instead grabbing one of his wrists, pushing his hand between us. His thumb glides over my clit, working it like an instrument. Plucking my strings like a tuned guitar.

Cassius may act the alpha part, but we both know the only alpha in this room is me.

I ride him with everything I have. Hate and lust and need powering my movements. My hips roll and my hands explore. They travel up his body, across torn stitches and scabbed over wounds. Wounds that I inflicted. I lean into him and let myself feel everything. My nails dig into his shoulder, my teeth bite at his nipple. Pleasure ripples through my body like electrical currents, propelling me up and down his length until I scream his name.

"I like the way my name sounds as you're coming."

I pull back to look at him, and an amused smile spreads across his face.

My fist introduces itself to his nose.

Blood gushes out of it.

His eyes narrow, and he thrusts his hips up. His cock is pressing on that delicious spot, and suddenly I'm in the air, Cassius lifting me as he stands. My back meets the couch with a thud as he pulls out of me. The absence of his cock has me clenching around nothing. He kicks off his shoes and pulls a condom out of the pants hanging precariously low around his hips. They drop to the floor at his feet, and he steps out of them.

His bloodied body gleams in the morning light. With the condom in place, he yanks my skirt from my body and enters me again in a single thrust. It's not tender or soft. He's rough and hard. Fast and angry. And it is all consuming. He presses his lips to mine, metallic and wet. His tongue forces its way into my mouth, and I greet it with enthusiasm.

An aggressive hand pulls at my shirt, dragging it up my

body, grazing a nipple as it passes. Cassius breaks our kiss to pull the shirt over my head, and his rhythm never falters. He hammers into me harder and harder, filling me to my core. Extending his arms fully, he changes the angle, and I wrap my legs around him, digging my heels into his ass. He thrusts faster, pushing me steadily towards the edge. My back arches and all the muscles in my legs tighten, as my orgasm rips through me, it seeps between us, coating us in desire.

Cassius pounds harder, faster, seeking his own release. I widen my legs, resting one on the back of the couch, and planting the other on the floor. Using the one on the floor, I slide a rogue throwing knife to my waiting hand and use my free one to drag my nails down his back. Then I press the blade into his throat, drawing a drop of blood.

Cassius bites his lip, his body tensing as he leans into my blade, filling the room with the most delicious, triumphant growl.

Dropping the knife, I swallow it with a kiss.

The look on his face as he came was as close as I'll ever get to heaven. But he's no angel, he's the devil, and we're a tangle of limbs and blood spiraling down into the pits of hell. I would never feel at home in heaven anyway. I'd much rather dance with the devil.

The emptiness I feel when he slips himself out of me is more real than anything I have ever felt. More real than watching the life slip from someone's eyes. More real than my enemies' blood swirling down the shower drain. My soul aches with every step he takes away from me. I am not sure what to think of this. Any of this. Of Cassius. Of me. Of the way he makes me feel. Wanted. Missed. Needed. Can I follow through with it? Killing him? And if I can't, what does that mean for me? For Ruby? For the Reds? For us? My breaths come faster, my heart beats erratically, panic settling in my chest. What have I done?

With the condom disposed of, Cassius grabs two bottles of water out of the small fridge in the corner of the room. He hands me one, and I sit up, my heart regulating itself. His mere presence quiets the panic. I open the water and bring it to my lips, swishing it around my mouth for a few seconds before swallowing.

His dark hair is mussed, and he eyes me suspiciously as he drains his water.

"Is my nose broken?" I ask him.

"Nah, I didn't hit you that hard." He nods his head toward me, his mouth pulled into a sly grin. "What about mine? Broken?"

"I didn't hit you that hard, either." I raise an eyebrow in response.

"You're covered in blood, and I don't know if it's yours or mine."

"Does it matter who it belongs to?"

"Is it weird that it doesn't?"

"I am not sure what to make of you, Cassius Cross," I tell him honestly.

He sits beside me on the couch and pulls me into him. I resist out of habit. My body reacting with violence, prodding the open wound on his thigh with my finger.

His lips press together in a grim line. "Ruby, let it fucking rest."

"I'm supposed to kill you."

"But we both know you won't."

"How can you be so certain?"

"Because we aren't strangers anymore. Because this shit between us is so electrifying it could power the city." With a soft touch to my chin, he turns me to face him. His stare sends shivers down my spine. I open my mouth to respond, but he continues. "Because even though I walked up those stairs with a plan to kill you, I would not have followed through with it. I needed to know what it felt like to be inside you. And now that I know—"

"I still want to kill you."

"But you won't. You think you're infallible, but you aren't. You falter for me. You stumble. You mess up. And you feel this too."

I shake my head, words escape me.

"I'm not invading your kingdom, Ruby. I have no intention of overthrowing your monarchy. I'm simply kneeling at your throne."

I pull away from him, his touch becoming too much. He stands and enters the bathroom attached to his office. Cassius lets his words hang in the air between us, floating over the broken room, the room we painted red with each other's blood. We are bleeding outside the lines, crossing barriers that aren't meant to be crossed.

When he comes back, he has a first aid kit. The smell of antiseptic blends into the smell of blood and sex. His wounds clean, he threads a needle and pushes it into his leg. If it hurts, he doesn't let it show. Red spots pepper the bronze hue of his skin as smears of blood dry on his handsome face. Evidence of our sins. Because that is what this is. A sin. A sin against the Reds. A sin against everything I stand for.

I coax the needle from his hand, pushing it through his skin and pulling it taut. Mending his wounds.

A sinner's repentance.

"What piece are you in this game?" I ask.

He tilts his head at me in confusion.

"The world is full of pawns. Weak pretenders. And knights? They walk the path less taken. They are unpredictable. A king though, he knows his place, he knows his weaknesses. Do you know yours, Cassius?"

"You." The word is a double-edged sword slicing through my armor.

I kiss him, tasting him like the secret he is. Naked truths pass between our lips.

Truths that could demolish a monarchy and assemble a kingdom from its ruins.

SEVENTEEN

My new chair creaks beneath my weight, not yet broken in. The smell of bleach lingers in the air. The only evidence Ruby was ever here are the fresh stitches on my leg and the tape over my broken nose. She was wrong, we both knew it.

The woman sitting across from me is trying to appear younger than she is, with heavy make-up and tight clothing. Wrinkles don't lie though; they play hide and seek at the corners of her eyes when she smiles. Which is what she's doing now, waiting for me to respond to her last comment. She's the kind of woman I would normally have had on their knees by now, begging for this job. Before. Before Ruby. It's been three days and there's been zero contact. Zero notes, calls, or clues. Nothing to hold onto.

"Mr. Cross?" the woman prods, her shoulders pushed back to give me a view of her ample cleavage. When I don't respond, she stands from her chair and takes up residence on my desk. Her tongue plays across her lips, attempting to entice me. But she's sitting on my desk. The same desk I had Ruby bent over only a few days ago. Black seeps into my vision, I wanted to bend her over it again, but now it's fucking tainted. Tainted by a woman whose name I can't remember and don't want to.

"Get the fuck out of my office." My words come out gruff through clenched teeth. All my effort going into not grabbing this woman by the throat and escorting her off my property. "You will never work here, and if I so much as see your face within one block of my club you will disappear, and nobody will ever find you." The threat is not an empty one, the threads of my calm composure are unraveling. Quickly.

I expect her to scramble off my desk, a mess of limbs and insecurities. Instead, she surprises me by sliding almost gracefully down from her perch. She adjusts her skirt as she heads toward the open door. Her long black ponytail swings with the sway of her hips. Before she crosses the threshold, she turns back to look at me, her lips pulled up on one side, inquisitive.

"Curious," she muses, her voice barely more than a whisper.

Tonight's games are well underway by the time I regain what little composure I have left. Most of the players are regulars, with a few I don't recognize mixed in. Nate hands me my tablet when I sit down, detailed profiles of the new players loaded courtesy of Garrett. They are thorough, listing family members, known associates, and assets.

I swipe through each one; the majority of new faces are young pricks gambling with mommy and daddy's money. They find out about the game through carefully crafted word of mouth. They come, they play, they get in over their heads, and I get mommy and daddy to clean up the mess. It's not a system I'm proud of, but it works.

I lean back in my chair and observe the games, the tells, the lies, the deceit, and the flirtation. A feminine hand grazes across a collar, her body hidden behind a young kid built like a linebacker. I bring him up on my tablet again. Fucking water polo playing pretentious prick. His profile pegs him as Bentley Drake, a sophomore at Marse University, home of the Pirates. Whose mascot is a fucking parrot—tell me how that makes sense? He's the son of Ashley and James Drake. Family money turned them into real estate moguls. I smile. If there's something I like more than money, it's property. Real estate is always a good idea.

Tilting my head up in a nod, I send Nate a silent question.

"She's not on G's—I mean Garrett's lists?" he asks, his voice so low only I can hear.

I shake my head. Her leg flicks up behind her when he pulls her into him, revealing a black heel with red bottoms. Jealousy pumps through my veins. I know those heels are a dime a dozen in a place like this, but it's too much of a coincidence. Who else could get in here without G knowing?

I hear her laugh, simple and completely fake. It sounds like how I imagine bubbles would laugh if they could. High-pitched and empty. Fragile.

I'm halfway to the craps table when her eyes meet mine. Her lips turn up in a smile that screams she's up to no good. She subtly brings a finger to her lips. Silently waving me off. He's a mark, the guy from the café. And watching her play with him sends all my blood rushing to my dick. Soft, loose, brunette curls hang down her back tonight. Her lips are painted a dark burgundy, not the red I've grown to love. Her cleavage spills over her dress every time she rolls the dice. It's black and tight, leaving nothing to the imagination.

And I want to rip it off her with my teeth.

"Bentley, is it?" I hold out my hand to the prick. "Cassius Cross. Welcome to the games. I hope they're proving to be worth your time."

The kid shakes my hand eagerly, a too large smile plastered on his face. *Stupid prick.* "Thanks man, it's nice to meet you. I've been hearing about these games for a while. Glad to finally have a chance to check them out."

"Looks like you're going to go home a winner either way," I say, making eye contact with Ruby.

I reach out my hand to her. "Cassius Cross."

"Lillian Cartwright, it's a pleasure to meet you." Her smile cuts me like a knife. Beautiful and dangerous. I'm done. Completely annihilated. The woman in front of me could wear a thousand disguises, and I would still know her. She could do anything she wanted to me, and I would let her. Her hand is so small in mine, but the squeeze she gifts me is larger than fucking life. Any life, even my own.

"She's my lucky charm tonight," Bentley announces, pulling her away from me and close to him again. "Come on baby, blow, and roll." He drops the dice in her hand.

Her long lashes flutter in amusement, but the smile she flashes at him doesn't reach her eyes.

"Good luck, kid," I say, stifling a laugh. Shamelessly wondering how much she'll make him suffer for that one.

I return to my chair by the door, leaving them to their game. I read the room like always, but my eyes only watch her. She's a master at misdirection, and only because I know that can I see what she's really doing. The way she leans into him at just the right moments to pour the contents of her drink into his. The way one hand always touches him. The hand that isn't touching him lifts her dress, fingering the knives strapped to her thigh.

Fuck me. And she does, with her eyes, every time she touches him. Every time he thinks he's winning, he's losing everything. She blows on the dice, her lips forming the perfect O, and then she licks them just for me. The need to touch her, to taste her, to breathe her in is so overwhelming. Fucking vixen.

I could shut down the games. I could lean her back on that poker table over there and taste every inch of her. I could ravish her body and sacrifice my own for her pleasure. I could. But I won't. I'm drowning without a life raft, and I don't give a flying fuck. I'm about to sink like the damn Titanic.

Her eyes are getting heavy, her movements sloppy. She slips out of one heel and falls into the kid, amber liquid spills from his glass. He looks down at her, and it's more than just the height difference. His eyes narrow. His jaw tightens. It's annoyance, and it's written all over his face.

Nate takes a step toward the table to defuse the situation. I shake my head. I want to see this play out.

She takes the cocktail napkin and uses it to pat the kid down. And down. And down. Until he's no longer annoyed. Now he's a fucking horny teenager instead. She pulls her bottom lip into her mouth, and the kid suddenly gets impatient. He can't leave soon enough. One arm full of chips and the other on her waist, he cashes out.

Barefoot, she drags him out the door.

One Mississippi, two Mississippi, three Mississippi.

"Boss?" Nate's voice interrupts.

Four Mississippi.

Nate opens his mouth to speak again.

I shake my head. Five Mississippi.

Fuck it.

I follow them.

I gave them enough of a head start that the kid doesn't know I'm here, but I would bet my entire existence that Ruby does. Her artificial giggles guide me through the maze of hallways, up the stairs, and out the back door.

The lot is dark, only a few lampposts illuminate the scene. His large body has her pinned against a car with one leg wrapped around him. I stay in the shadows, hidden from everyone but her. He moves a hand to her thigh, but she pushes it away in a flurry of movement. His body jerks. He stumbles backwards, his hands move to his throat. Dark pools begin to form at his feet. The prick falls, crumbling like Rome at the hands of a barbarian. A beautiful fucking barbarian.

She offers me a small shrug and then uses the side view mirror to apply the red lipstick I've come to love so much. Leaning over the kid, still gurgling with life, she speaks to him. I strain to hear, but am unsuccessful. His body slows, his movements sluggish. An eternity passes as we both wait for him to still.

She stands, stepping into the light, showcasing the splatters in shades of red that coat her body. Then the artist looks back at her masterpiece, and signs it with a kiss.

Eighteen

Sometimes I lie underwater in my bathtub until my chest feels like it's going to cave in. Until every molecule of oxygen has been exhausted. Until I sit on the brink of death. The plane of existence between life and death is where I hold my secrets. Where my sins haunt me, and my past comes out to play.

The moments after I surface, the ones where I gasp for air? That's when I feel lightest, when I feel most alive.

I expected the air in the Impala to be thick and hard to swallow, but it's exactly the opposite. I didn't know it was possible to feel alive without first knocking on death's door, but here I am, and I've never felt more alive in my life. The air feels new somehow, lighter, like if I breathe too fast, I could float away.

Cassius does not speak for most of the drive, but he doesn't need to. He feels it too. The shift in the air. The shift into the unknown. He looks at me, and I look at him, and it's joyful. It's happiness. It's fearless. It's right.

Even if it is wrong.

His grip is tight on the gear shift, the veins in his forearm prominent. I trace one with my finger, and his jaw hardens, calling to me. A siren's song. I kneel in my seat, desperate to answer the call. Leaning into him, I press my lips into the soft spot below his chin. His pulse quickens beneath my touch, and I want him to touch me. I want him to feel how he jumpstarts my pulse too. How I was once dead and am now resurrected.

He shifts gears, and I am rewarded when his knuckles quickly brush between my thighs. The sense of loss is immediate, and a whimper escapes me when they don't return.

A rumble builds in his chest, vibrating up his throat until a deep growl emerges. His nostrils flare. Gravel flies. My body quakes. And his primal display sends my hormones into overdrive. The car comes to a halting stop, and my body lurches toward the windshield, only stopped short by the strong arm braced in front of me. My fingers move of their own accord to my thigh, the cold steel of the blade offering comfort.

Cassius puts the car in park, his eyes never leaving mine. His hands wrap around my waist, and he lifts me onto his lap. Straddling him, I feel his arousal through his slacks. He leans forward, and then his seat falls backwards, forcing us to lay down. The tip of my blade draws blood from his throat. A strong hand grabs my wrist, squeezing until the knife falls from my grasp.

His gray eyes narrow, and his jaw clenches. His practiced hands slide up my hips, my dress rising with them. Fingers dig into me hard enough that I expect I will see bruises in the mirror later. I reach for his zipper, but instead he pulls me up his body and I scramble to support myself, my body lurching forward. My hands seek refuge on the backseat headrest, and I let my knees fall to either side of his face.

His tongue slides through my folds, light as a feather. A soft tingling works its way through me as he flicks his tongue around my clit, never hitting the spot I need.

Fucking tease.

I groan in frustration, and he nips at me.

Fuck.

He works his tongue deeper, like I'm his last meal and he can't get enough. I'm about to go over the edge, but he stops to suck on my clit. My hips buck, I need more. His hands slide over my ass, rough and authoritative. The scruff on his chin scratches the inside of my thigh and my God do I like it. He could kill me right here, and I would die on the top of the world.

I bite my lip to keep from crying out, afraid he'll stop.

A finger joins his tongue, and he works them in tandem. Two fingers slide in and out of my pussy, harder and faster. His tongue works feverishly at my clit. The world starts to fade. He slides his other hand through my wetness, dragging it between my cheeks, priming me. He twirls a finger around my puckered hole and pushes it inside.

His hands move expertly, filling me up, building the pressure. His teeth graze me, and I come undone, my legs quake and tighten until I am paralyzed with pleasure and the dam breaks. Somewhere, mirrors break from my cries. Warmth pools between my legs.

I'm shattered. Maybe never to be put back together.

Cassius nips at my inner thigh and then slides me down his chest before lifting me back into the passenger seat. He drags his hand down his face, slick with evidence of me. His normally perfect hair is an unkempt mess, the short strands loose from their typical hold. I think I catch a glimpse of a smile, but it disappears faster than it registers.

He doesn't say a word, just adjusts his erection and then his seat. He leans out the window, and it is only then that I see where we are. The Impala purrs to life, and we pull through the open gates and up the driveway to his home.

I don't know if it's the effect of a mind-blowing orgasm or my current love of life, but the stars in the sky are brighter, the smell of the night wind is sweeter, and the sound of Cassius snarling is the most beautiful music I have ever heard.

NINETEEN

S he fucking cut me open again. I don't open the door for her. I don't wait for her to climb out of the car. I don't signal for her to come inside.

The front door slams behind me, echoing in the empty night.

Pressing my back against the wall, I wait. Suspense and need boil over all my edges.

I never really understood the phrase silence is deafening.

Until now.

Nothingness. Emptiness. A cavern of quiet.

I strain to hear something, anything, but I can't even hear the sound of my own breathing.

Eternity. That's what this is.

Disappointment cloaks me.

Defeated, I open the door.

Nothing.

She's gone.

Vanished.

I thought she was the captain of the ship, but now I see she's the iceberg.

TWENTY

"Our client wants to know why Mr. Cross is not dead yet," Rowan hisses at me, struggling to keep up. "And the rest of the Reds are starting to ask questions. It's been weeks and he's not even on the schedule yet."

"Do we know who hired us?" I ignore the rest of her statements, keeping pace to put distance between us and the rest of the reds exiting the meeting.

"Anonymous."

"Not really, though, right?"

"I dug Rubes, whoever wants him dead covered their tracks," she hesitates, "and, they completed the objective."

I pause to look at her, not following.

She pulls my braid from behind my back, a red ribbon

tied in a perfect bow on the end. It's not a coincidence that the first meeting Alice attends is the meeting in which they succeed. There are no coincidences in life. Only fate.

Fate can either lift you up or bring you to your knees, which is exactly where I find myself ten minutes later. The smallest Amelia stands in front of me with a wooden training blade in her hand. Her movements are jerky and unpolished, but we'll get there.

"You must think of your blade as an extension of you," I tell the girls, rising to my feet. "It is part of you, as if your hand has been replaced with hilt and steel."

A middle Amelia stabs at the dummy in front of her, her body stiff.

"We are women. We are graceful. Killer ballerinas. Light on our feet and fluid." I pull my knife from its sheath on my thigh. The room spins, the earth stills. I stand behind the dummy, my blade at its throat and my eyes on Alice. See me. Be me.

She twirls, her blonde hair fanning around her. When she comes to a stop she lunges forward and then loses balance and falls.

The oldest of the girls laughs, and the others follow.

Alice offers the girl a smile, but the smile is a warning that only I see. She raises her arm behind her, the training knife soars through the air. There are gasps and then a cry as blood pours from Amelia's nose. The rest of the Amelia's stop laughing. Alice is doubled over in giggles.

"You," I say pointing at Alice, "stay here. The rest of you take Amelia down to Rosalie."

The girls shuffle quickly and silently out of the training

facility, leaving me alone with Alice.

"Where did you learn to do that?"

She shrugs her shoulders. "You learn to do a lot of things when you're bored. No TV to watch, no video games to play. And you don't go to school 'cause the teachers ask too many questions."

I hand her another training knife. "This time hit the target over there."

She takes the knife from my hand, brings it back and sends it hilt over blade into the target. The hilt hits the bullseye, and the knife tumbles to the floor.

I take one of the throwing knives off the hook on the wall. She takes it eagerly and weighs it in her hand. She brings the knife back, throws it, and the blade sinks into the bullseye.

"Again," I say, handing her another one.

She does it again.

I hand her another, but this time I instruct her to throw it at the dummy and to hit him in center chest.

She does as she is told. Remarkable is an understatement.

"Pick up that sparring blade." She picks it up. Touches the blade across her fingers. She's not scared of it. She's intrigued, curious even.

"Slice his throat."

She moves silently, like she must have in the meeting, like I witnessed the night I saved her. Soft on her feet, sure of her steps, she reaches the dummy, but fumbles with the knife. The tip hits the dummy in the shoulder and bounces off, sending Alice sprawling.

I offer her my hand, but she shakes me off.

"Tell me," I say, "How did you do it? Those girls have

been trying for weeks."

"It was so easy when you were all looking at the screen. I just had to wait until nobody was looking. Besides, the other girls, they're too loud, and they don't know how to wait. They just move quickly to try and get things over with. Sometimes you need to move slowly to not be seen."

So much wisdom in such a little girl. Maybe she should be teaching stealth. She attempts to slice the dummy's throat again, only this time she moves with the practice blade in her hand, its hilt shoved down the sleeve of her shirt.

Be one with the blade. She repeats this method over and over again, flawlessly.

She could have been a dancer. A real dancer. She could have curtsied on stage and had flowers thrown at her feet.

Instead, she dances with death.

TWENTY-ONE

"D o you have a plan?" Garrett helps himself to a glass of bourbon and sits across from me. He swirls the amber liquid in the glass, sniffing it as it spins.

"Dude, what the fuck are you doing?"

"Huh?"

"We grew up on six-dollar vodka. Don't sit there and pretend to know what you're doing with that." I throw a coaster at him.

He clutches his chest. "Says the guy who just threw a fucking coaster at me."

"And a plan? Other than killing the person who hired her? No."

"Do you really think it was him?"

"Do we know anyone else stupid enough to pull this shit?"

Garrett shakes his head. Because we don't. Nobody else would. I don't have enemies. And while my life hasn't been perfect, I've protected those who needed it. Garrett included. And I've killed anyone who has been even a miniscule threat. Except for the loose thread I should have dealt with months ago. But I didn't want the heat, so I backed off. Not anymore.

Garrett picks up his knight and moves it to F3.

"Remind me why I play this game with you?" I groan.

"Because it keeps our minds sharp?"

Mine has never been as sharp as Garrett's, but until recently, I'd always been able to hold my own with him. Stress eats at me, so I'm not surprised that I'm not in the right headspace for this right now, besides my mind has been a million miles away since...

I clear my throat and crack my neck.

"Yours, maybe," I say as I slide one of my pawns forward.

"So focus man. Chess is what we used to do when shit got real. It's relaxing. Stop stressing," he says as his knight attacks my pawn, sacrificing itself.

He's right though; I know he's right. Using my pawn, I attack his knight. Chess is where we used to hide. It's where everything was right and safe. When we couldn't go home, we'd go to old man Forrest's and play chess. We would sit on his front porch for hours, getting eaten alive by mosquitos and drinking sun tea. The tea was awful, but the game wasn't. Forrest taught us everything he knew about chess, including how to read your opponent and how to think several moves ahead.

When we started regularly smoking his ass, Forrest taught us poker and, more importantly, how to count cards. Garrett and I can both count, but G can't mask his features. So while he took to the counting, it was the deceit he struggled with. We owe that old man everything. Which is why he spent the last days of his life in a cushy nursing home, and his granddaughter wants for nothing—even if neither of them knows why or how. It's better that way. Our past has to stay in the past.

"Did she break your brain too?" Garrett gestures to my face. "Or just your nose?"

"It was worth it." And it was. I would spend hours trying to read whatever game board her and I are playing on if it gave me one more taste of her. Because this game we're playing, it far surpasses the ones that came before.

"It's your turn, jackass."

My fingers rest on what has quickly become my most important chess piece, and I consider her move.

My queen. Ruby. Are they not one and *the* same?

My phone buzzes on the table with an incoming text.

"Saved by the vibration," Garrett mumbles and leans back in his chair, crossing his arms in clear annoyance. "Let me guess, it's the crazy bitch looking for a booty call?"

> Nate: Package delivered.

"Actually, no. But it's something almost as good. And besides, we both know you were going to win."

I leave him to his sulking.

Twenty-Two

"The girls are already speculating."

I do not turn to face Riley. Instead, I keep my focus on the training mat, where the Amelia's practice hand-to-hand combat with Rawlings. Alice ducks, barely avoiding a fist.

"I just thought you should know," she continues. "She's very bright and an excellent student. She seems to pick up on everything easily. Like it's in her nature. Part of her physical and emotional make up."

Turning my head, I look at Riley.

"Like you, I mean." She casts her eyes down, unable to hold my gaze.

"Like me."

"I just, Ruby… you might not want to wait. That's all I'm saying." Riley's voice drops to a barely audible whisper, "Unless you do, and Ruby, I'd stand behind you on that."

I turn back to the girls, the sound of Riley's steps getting further and further away.

We speculated too. Well, the other girls did, for years before I was named. Rowan and I never offered our opinion, but we listened to the others. We couldn't decide if me being Ruby was a good thing or a bad thing. The older girls seemed jealous of my skill, but it also seemed like so much pressure to put on a young girl.

And Rowan and I were both so young. Young enough to be afraid of what was going on around us, and old enough to understand it was a better alternative than where we came from. We held each other those first few nights when the shadows crept in and settled around us, cloaking us in their darkness. It was one we were unfamiliar with, but we quickly realized that we could hide there. Our pasts, our pain, could stay in the darkness where nobody else had to see it. It was just us. Us against the world.

It didn't take long to see why Rowan was recruited to be a Red. If the high court knew how good she was on computers back then, I imagine she would have been shipped out to serve under another Ruby as a young teen. She had far surpassed her instructor's skills by then. Computers are Rowan's second, if not first, language. But I think Ruby wanted Rowan for herself, just like she wanted me. Or maybe in some sick way she wanted my only friend to be nearby but just out of reach. The friend I was no longer allowed to have, allowed to confide in. We were separated, only allowed to speak to each other if another red commanded it. Ruby's own special form of torture, just another way to break me.

"Ruby! Watch out!" Rawlings shouts as two Amelias tumble toward me, a mess of hair and black spandex.

"Enough," I yell, and the two girls separate and climb to their feet. Their hair is a mess, sticking out of their braids, and Alice's nose is bleeding. The other girl rubs her scalp, eyes narrowed at Alice. Alice gives me an upside-down smile and then holds her hand out to the girl who stands there unmoving. Alice opens her fist and hair floats to the floor.

"You," I point to Alice. "Follow me. Now."

I turn on my heel and a chorus of "Oohs" hit my back.

"Ten laps for the rest of them," I yell over my shoulder to Rawlings.

"You heard the queen. Get running, brats."

Halfway down the hall, I have to turn around to make sure Alice is behind me. She is—smug smile and all. Her footsteps are so light, it almost makes me uneasy. Part of me wants to force her to walk in front of me.

I lead her inside an empty training room. The stretching room that the Reds lovingly refer to as the torture chamber. She stands in the middle of the room, her eyes watching me as I move closer. It's on the tip of my tongue, everything Ruby said to me that first day. I even open my mouth, but then close it again. She doesn't move as I pace the room. She doesn't speak to fill the silence. She waits. Is she afraid? Or is she anticipating praise? I can't tell.

"You," I start. I need to do this, it's my legacy, but the girl in front of me is just that, a little girl. One who needs people that love her and take care of her. People who build her up, not break her down. Just because she was handed a shit life, doesn't mean she has to live mine.

I don't know if I can do this.

"I... I don't think you are Ruby material," I say, and her face pinches. "I don't think you have it in you, despite what the other girls are saying."

"But," she blubbers. "But..."

"But, nothing." I deliver my final blow and leave her in the torture chamber, slamming the door behind me. There's something I have to do.

Now.

TWENTY-THREE

"**I**t wasn't me; I swear."

The man struggles against his restraints, while I struggle against myself. I've never been one for restraints. I've always preferred the back and forth of fists, the bounce in my feet. The adrenaline. I don't know why I thought this was a good idea. As if I wasn't pent-up before, Ruby ghosting me has me coiled up so tight I can feel my blood pumping against my skin.

Expand.

Contract.

Expand.

Contract.

"You can't kill me," the man says sternly. "I know people.

They'll find you."

Expand.

Contract.

Expand

Contract.

"Just let me go, I won't tell anyone."

Expand.

Contract.

My knuckles connect with his jaw, knocking his head off its axis. Blood and saliva fly from his lips, spraying the floor. A tooth bounces along the tile until it finally comes to a stop near Nate's foot. The man's head hangs, his bald spot on full display. The overhead light shines, casting a glare.

Nate hits him with the hose.

Wake up motherfucker.

The man's head lolls. I nod to Nate. Another blast of water.

One eye opens and then another, his head lifts.

"You're going to rot in jail," he spurts. Blood coats what's left of his teeth.

Expand.

Contract.

Manic laughter bubbles into the air, and Elijah Cranston smiles. It's a loser's smile. A dying man's smile.

I pick up the staple gun off the table, and pull the trigger a few times, sending staples flying in his direction.

His face slackens, all composure abandoned.

"Please," he slobbers. "I didn't hire her. I swear on my kid's lives."

Expand.

Contract.

"You mean the kid who tortured Isabella? That kid?"

"He didn't! I swear!"

"You took a teenage girl into foster care, and then adopted her so that your piece of shit son could have a plaything. Do you know what the bones in the human body sound like when they are crushed by a ton of speeding metal?"

Elijah blubbers, tripping over his own lies as he tries to get the words out of his mouth.

The table of tools calls to me like it always does. When my fingers graze the sledgehammer, Elijah pulls in a hard breath.

"This one?" I lift the sledgehammer to give him a better view. It's heavy in my hands, but a good heavy. A familiar one. It's like an old, worn T-shirt, the one with all the holes that you can't seem to throw away. It's a part of you. The wooden handle looks and feels scarred like me.

A smile creeps over my face. I'm like a kid in a goddamn candy store.

"Nate! Nate! He wants this one." I hold the hammer up for his approval.

He only grunts in response. I can never tell if he wants to laugh and is afraid, or if I'm not funny. Oh, well.

I lift the hammer over my head, bringing it down on Elijah's knee.

Screams fill the room, echoing off the soundproof walls.

"You son of a bitch! It wasn't me!"

"Maybe paralyzing Junior wasn't enough. Maybe I should put him down too."

His expression droops. "I know who hired her," he

mumbles. With his admission, his face comes back to life, the skin pulling taut over his features.

But I don't even care at this point if he knows anything about who hired Ruby. His wife and daughters deserve better. Isabella deserved better.

The hammer drops to my feet, the metal hitting the concrete with a thunk that reverberates around us. The knife I pick up to replace it is unfamiliar and I hold it in the light to admire it. The silver blade gleams. It's not a tool I normally use. It's delicate where I am rough, creating art in places one would not normally expect. But I'm not an artist. Not yesterday, not today. I lack the patience, the finesse.

I shove the knife all the way to the hilt into Elijah's kidney. With the handle tight in my grip, I twist. His screams sound like music to my ears.

Expand.

Contract.

The red fades to black, all the anger that's built up over the last few weeks comes to a head, clouding my vision and my thoughts.

A strong hand grabs my arm, bringing the world back into focus.

The room is painted red, I don't remember it, but the carnage is palpable. Cranston's blood coats every surface of the room, the floor is slick beneath my feet. What's left of him is unrecognizable as it falls unceremoniously to the floor, a mess of muscle and flesh. I'm not a chef like Ruby, slicing and dicing. I'm a fucking butcher.

Dropping the knife, I look at Nate. He nods and I walk up the stairs to my office, leaving him to do what he does best.

Cleaning up my messes.

Twenty-Four

The bodies that lay on either side of me are still warm. She's in a tank and panties, he's in boxers. I don't know where her blood ends and his begins. It's a blanket tucked around the three of us. A warm cocoon of death.

Tears slide down my cheeks, diluting the blood that stains them. Crying is as unfamiliar to me as the people I lay between. But the tears keep falling; I can't make them stop.

Soulless Ruby. You are supposed to be soulless.

I rub my hand to my chest, trying to ease the pressure threatening to crush me. It's like someone is sitting on top of me, and I imagine it's the ghost of eight-year-old me coming to witness what I should have done eighteen years ago.

This would not have been an issue before. Before him.

Before Cassius, I would have pirouetted through the puddles of blood and used their intestines in a private ribbon twirl routine. But instead, I lay here broken, weak.

Fuck him.

Fuck him for all of this. This is all his fault. How can one person break you and put you back together? Is it possible to be the torturer and the savior?

I slip out of the bed. I do not kiss them. This kill was not Ruby's. This kill was for eight-year-old Ember and her baby sister staring at her through the bars of her crib.

"I'm not sorry," I tell her. "I'm only sorry I didn't do it sooner."

In the hallway, an orange tabby cat chews on a woman's bare scalp. It pauses to look at me as I step over the woman's body. She had tried to run. They always try to run. The scalping was a pure accident. I have never done that before, but when she ran, I grabbed her by the hair and one thing led to another and well, here we are.

Red paw prints lead me down the hall, back to the kitchen and living room. A dozen dead eyes look up at me from the floor, their bodies surrounded by filth. Some things never change. Pools of blood spread, congealing around trash and cat feces. It blooms like spring flowers on the bread of a moldy sandwich on the counter. Next to it lays a bent spoon.

Cries carry from the back bedroom. Will she survive this? Will the baby be forced to live with the effects of this life until this point? She looked small in her crib, but I don't really know babies, so maybe that's the size she's supposed to be? I do know that I can't stay. I can't help her any more than this.

I hope that eight-year-old me is proud, that she sees this

as a triumph. As a way to balance the scales. I hope that hunger pains no longer haunt her. Nor the fear of strangers in her home. I hope she's healthy and normal.

Fucking normal.

This is so far from fucking normal. I am so far from fucking normal. Fuck eight-year-old me. She's a little wimp. She was so fucking useless. Nobody loved her. Nobody cared what happened to her, she didn't even care what happened to herself. And she deserved it. All of it. The neglect, the pain, because she was weak.

Closing the door, I take my phone out of my boot and call Rowan.

"Get CPS here now. The baby is crying."

"Got it Rubes, you okay?"

I don't know how to answer her, my world is fuzzy. Bleeding over my edges. Pooling outside my comfort zone.

All I can do is hang up. I'm not okay. Nothing is okay, and a single face is my tipping point.

Cassius.

Getting on my bike, I ride into the night.

Only one of us can walk away from this.

TWENTY-FIVE

The sound of shattering glass wakes me, followed by a blood-curdling scream. My heart hammers in my chest as the noises register. I sit up in bed and reach for the gun I keep in my bedside drawer.

"Cassius," Ruby screeches from the stairs. "Cassius!"

I look down at the gun in my hand. I want to think this is a game, but she sounds different, she sounds human. Her voice, normally robotic and deadpan, sounds thick with emotion. Despair and elation battle with each syllable of my name.

Seconds pass, long seconds where the only sound is the beating of my heart, ominous in the dark of the night. Ruby rounds the doorway of my bedroom, and the woman that stands before me is anything but human. She's a monster. I don't have to see the red hues to know that it's blood that covers her. Her long hair is matted in stringy dreads. Her face could be confused for a Jackson Pollock.

She tilts her head to the side with a quick jerk—the movement terrifying. Up until now, I haven't been afraid. Scared, yeah, but a good scared. The kind of scared that makes shit exciting. Thrilling. I'm a thrill seeker, and she's been my roller coaster. But right now, in this very moment, I think she might actually try to kill me.

I rustle the blankets to muffle the sound of the safety.

She's quiet. Too quiet. She pulls up her lips into a strange smile, her eyes widen, and the whites make her look even more sinister. Suddenly, she springs to life, throwing her body at me. The silver of the blade in her hand glitters in the moonlight.

I'm ready for her though and my hand snags her wrist, preventing her attack. The dagger clatters to the floor. Her eyes go wide and wild with rage. She brings her other hand to my throat, but her movements are slow, and it catches us both by surprise. We tumble off the bed, a mess of limbs and sheets. In the chaos, the gun becomes an obstacle, and her teeth sink into my wrist, causing the gun to slip from my fingers, lost in the bedding that ensnares us.

I pull myself free, almost falling in the process. Frantically, I search for the gun, but it's so dark, all I can see is a mess of shadows at my feet. Suddenly, Ruby scrambles to all fours, then clambers to her feet, holding my gun in her trembling hands.

"You did this to me," she screams. "You!" Her hand

shakes as she lifts the gun, pointing the barrel at my chest. "This is all your fucking fault." Tears stream down her face.

"Come on, baby," I plead, knowing the risk. "Give me the gun. You don't want to shoot me." I take a step toward her, closing the distance between us. The barrel of the gun presses into my sternum, but I believe what I said. The tears say more than her words. She doesn't want to shoot me. She won't.

"I was fine before you," she whispers. "I liked my life. I was content with it. And then you..." the gun digs deeper, "you came and fucked it all up. You fucked me all up. Tonight was supposed to be easy. Killing them was not supposed to hurt, Cassius. Why did it fucking hurt?"

I wrap my hand around the barrel of the gun and push it sideways. Her grip loosens, and I take it from her. Making quick work of releasing the magazine, I clear the chamber before I drop the pieces on the bed.

"Why did it fucking hurt?" she repeats. "It's all your fault." She pounds one fist into my chest, and then the other. I let her. I don't know what's happening with her, but I let her take it out on me. I wrap her in my arms and let her hit me until she's finally had enough. Until all the fight has left her, and she's only a shell of the woman I've come to know.

I lead her to the bathroom and gently remove her clothes. I put myself between her and the mirror and when she tries to look around me, I pull her focus back to me. I'm afraid of the picture she'll see in the blood that paints her.

"Just you and me, babe, okay?" I keep my voice gentle, but she cries harder. "I've got you," I tell her, and I pull her to my chest. Pressing a kiss to her matted hair, I whisper, "I've got you."

We climb into the shower, and I wash her hair until the water runs clear. She tries to look down, but I use my knuckle to lift her chin, forcing her to look at me. "Just you and me," I repeat.

I use a cloth to clean the dried blood from her body. I try to be gentle, but some areas must be older than others, like she took her time. So I scrub in gentle circles. My hard dick brushes against her thigh when I move to clean her back, and her gaze flickers to it and then back to me just as fast.

I shake my head. "Ruby, you're beautiful and naked," I say sheepishly. "But that's not what's happening right now, okay?"

"Ember," she whispers.

I pause mid-scrub. "What's ember?"

"My name." Her eyes focus on mine. "My real name. I became Ruby when I was recruited to replace the Ruby before me."

"The Ruby before you?"

"We're the Loyal Reds. We have kingdoms in several countries. I am the queen of this one. Our kingdom is small, there's only nine of us including me, plus a few recruits."

When I don't respond, she continues, "I was only eight when I was recruited. My parents were drunks. I learned to be soft on my feet so that I wouldn't disturb them. If I did, they would lock me in my room for what felt like days. I was so little, it seemed like forever. They would sell their food stamps for half the cash and then buy beer or liquor. I had to steal food to survive."

"I had to steal food too," I admit solemnly, but I do not

elaborate. Instead, I wrap her in my warmth. The spray of the shower falling around us.

"My predecessor watched me steal food for two months before she recruited me. She taught me to become detached, numb, and immune to emotions and death. And I was."

"Until me," I say.

"Until you," she confirms.

"It was them you killed tonight, wasn't it?" I ask. "Your parents?"

"Yes. The pieces of shit just had another baby about a year ago. I couldn't let it continue."

I shut off the water and grab a towel from the hook. Taking my time, I dry her body, committing every curve to memory in case this was only a slip in judgment for her and I never get another chance. She's so beautiful, in the kind of way that hurts your soul. The kind of hurt that's so bad it's good. The kind that leaves you willing to bleed for more. God above, Devil below, Greek Gods, and every other higher power I can't remember right now, whoever is listening, please give me more. Please don't let this be the last. I want more. I need more.

I climb into a pair of boxers and hand Ruby a T-shirt. She pulls it over her head and wrings out her hair with the towel a second time. Her fingers comb through the red strands, twisting pieces until it's in a neat braid. With the end held tightly between her lips, she pulls off a piece of dental floss from the spool on the counter and ties it around the end.

Taking her hand, we climb into bed. I pull her close to me and wait. I wait for her to pull away, to run away, to leave. I wait for anything to happen, and everything to happen. But then her breathing evens out, her heartbeat slows, and I start to relax. My body loosens, my heartbeat skips to match hers, until sleep overtakes me too.

TWENTY-SIX

Morning seeps into the room, filtered through the blinds. A warm arm wraps around me, pulling me to rest on his chest.

Cassius.

Everything is so heavy, my limbs, my thoughts, my life. My parents are dead. My mark is taking care of me. Where once I stood in darkness alone, I am now blanketed in safety and light.

I trail a finger down an old scar on his chest. It's not one I put there. It's crescent shaped and jagged, so faded that had I not been this close, I probably wouldn't have noticed it.

"I was twelve," he says softly, answering the question I didn't ask. His voice is hoarse with sleep, rough around the quiet edges. "My mom had a new flavor of the week. She had this grand idea of a knight in shining armor who would come to save her. A man who would give her everything money could buy including a one-way ticket out of the Row."

I look up at him quizzically.

"The Row, that's what they call the part of town I grew up in. At one point, I guess when my great-grandparents bought their house for pennies on the dollar, it was a nice area, but drugs and violence eventually seeped their way into the neighborhood. Almost everyone knew someone on death row. I guess someone must have said it once and it stuck."

"Anyway," he continues, "my mom did everything she could to get out of the Row, except the things that would actually get her out of there, like work. She had a new boyfriend every week, a new fiancé every month. Most of them would knock me around, but very few ever got rough with her. My mom was a crazy fucking bitch."

He tugs gently at my braid. "She'd give you a real run for your money."

His chest rumbles beneath me with laughter, and I decide it's the best sound I've ever heard.

"So, I was twelve and this dude, he was huge, much bigger than me at the time, and probably even bigger than me now, went after Garrett. G had told him he was wrong about something, I don't even remember what, but this dude dove over the kitchen table and had his hands around G's neck. I jumped on the guy's back and started wailing at him with anything I could reach. A cookie sheet, a spatula, and finally a coffee mug. After I hit him over the head with it, it vibrated in my hand so hard I dropped it. The dude let go of G, tore me off his back and threw me across the house. I landed on the coffee table in the living room, chest down on a stupid pewter Lord of the Rings ashtray. Fucking thing was covered in elves." He chuckles. "And those elves were sharp."

"Oh my God," I say, trying to keep the laughter out of my voice, but it creeps slowly up my spine until I can't hold it in any longer. I'm shaking with laughter. "You were literally attacked by elves."

His hand brushes a loose strand of hair out of my face. "I think that's the first time I've ever heard you laugh." His lips press into the top of my head. "I like it."

"I didn't know you and Garrett had been friends for so long."

"We've been friends since we were like... seven? Maybe eight? He and his dad moved in next door. We spent a lot of time at my house because at least at my house there was only a chance of getting our ass beat. My mom may have been a crazy bitch, but his dad was cruel. We were left on our own a lot, so we did a lot of stealing. Looking back, I don't know if we were as good at it as we thought we were. I wonder if the lady at the corner bodega just felt bad."

I turn, resting my chin on his chest. His smile is bright and warm, and I'm not sure how it's possible that it's both. Bright is harsh, warm is soft. He's a contradiction. I reach up, my fingertips slide down his face, committing his jawline to memory. He swallows and his eyes search mine.

"She's alive."

I sit up.

"She's safe."

"Cassius, what do you mean she's alive?"

"The girl. The one you're looking for."

"How?" I climb out of bed; the floor is cold under my bare feet. How did he do it? And better yet, how did Rowan miss it?

"Garrett helped, he's really good at what he does."

"Rowan is too."

"Rowan?"

"She is my tech person." I stop pacing. "And I think she might be my best friend. My only friend."

"Well, in your BFF's defense, I actually did kidnap her. I had to make it look real. But then we set her up in a safe place far away from here."

"But why did you do it?"

"Babe, she was trafficked by her own father. He sold her to Elijah Cranston. You know, the big shot defense attorney? He's dead, by the way. Anyway, he legally adopted her. Which only made it worse. She was a gift for his fucking piece of shit son."

I groan. "Cassius, what did you do?"

"I assumed it was him who hired you and if anyone deserved to die it was that douchebag. Besides, you pissed me off, leaving me here high and dry the other night. I had to get my aggression out somehow."

I level him with a glare. "Wait, you are blaming me for this?"

"Damn right," he counters as he climbs out of bed, his long strides reaching me in no time.

"Cassius, how the hell is this my fa—"

His lips cut me off. His kiss feels like it wants to swallow me in a single bite. He's a ravenous beast and I'm his prey. He pulls away, his eyebrows narrow.

"Get on your knees," he commands.

When I don't move, his eyes darken, but his voice quiets. It's so low that I almost miss when he says, "What did I tell you before? You may be a queen out there, but this," his finger jabs the air between us, "this is my fucking kingdom. Get on your fucking knees and don't make me repeat myself in the bedroom ever again."

My insides squirm and I bite my bottom lip. "I think—"

Cassius growls, and that is all it takes to bring me to my knees. Thoughts? What fucking thoughts?

He pulls down his boxers, gripping his length. He strokes it once, twice, three times. The veins in his forearm throb. When he releases himself, pre-cum glistens the tip as it stares me in the face.

"Lick it," Cassius commands, and there can be no mistaking the moisture between my legs or the fire building inside me. I don't consider myself inexperienced, but I wonder if it's possible for Cassius to make me come with just his voice. I wouldn't be against testing that theory and I want to say so, but his eyebrows raise in a silent challenge, and I turn my head away from him.

His hands grab either side of my head, forcing me back to center. He releases my head and wraps one hand around my braid, pulling it tight. Gaining control.

"I said, lick it," Cassius repeats. Hard consonants punctuating each word.

I grip his cock in my hand and flatten my tongue on the underside of his shaft, sliding it down to the base. I take my time getting back to the tip, grazing him with my teeth. This fucker wants to play, I'll play.

The grip on my hair tightens. I try to pull myself off him, but he holds me in place. My eyes shift up to his. His are closed, but his jaw is clenched, his eyebrows pinched. I can't tell if it's pleasure or anger. Before I can contemplate that longer, his eyes flash open.

"Look at me and do it again," Cassius demands through gritted teeth.

I hold my eyes on his. Full of hellfire, and I'm an unapologetic sinner. Again, I flatten my tongue on the underside of his dick, grazing him with my teeth on the retreat. But this time, when I get to the tip, I swirl my tongue around the head. He licks his lips and then without warning he shoves inside my mouth, forcing me to gag.

"Mmm, I love that sound," he admits without breaking eye contact.

Fuck me.

I stroke him and suck him in tandem, working his full length. I graze him with my teeth just to see him tense. He never pulls my hair, but he uses his grip to force himself deep. Cassius buries himself in my throat. My insides quake, and my pussy aches for attention. Gripping his balls with one hand, I hollow out my cheeks and suck harder. His eyes darken and his body tenses, but he doesn't come. I do it again. His eyes close, breaking our connection, and his jaw hardens.

"Not. Yet," he says.

I do it again.

He pulls my mouth off his cock so fast, it makes a pop sound.

"Up," he orders. "Get on the bed. Now."

When I stand, my legs feel wobbly, weak with desire. I sit on the edge of the bed waiting to be told what to do and I would do almost anything for him to touch me right now. But he doesn't say anything. He twirls a finger in the air, his face stone. I flip over onto my knees with my back to him. In one swift movement, he's pulled two pillows beneath my hips and pushed my face to the mattress. He holds my wrists at the base of my back, his grip tight.

He slides a finger through my folds, and I bite the inside of my cheek trying to hold back a moan but fail. Cassius touches me again. This time, when he gets to my clit, he teases it. Small, light flicks. My body squirms beneath him. I need more. Faster. Harder.

Give me more, Cassius.

"Looks like my queen likes being told what to do." his finger rubs quickly but gently, and my knees try to close of their own accord. "You're so wet for me, baby." His voice is low, seducing me with every word. My back arches, lifting my ass closer to him, inviting him to push me harder, give me more. The bed envelopes my face and my shoulders, and I have to adjust myself to breathe.

Cassius removes his hand from my clit and replaces it with his cock, gliding along my folds, but never giving me the release I need. He pushes his fingers between my lips, forcing me to taste myself, while at the same time shifting the blankets away from my nose and mouth.

Moans fill the air and for a second, I wonder where they're coming from. But it's me. I'm moaning around his fingers while his hard cock slides between my ass cheeks.

"If you don't stop with the noises, I'm going to come a

lot faster than I planned," he says quietly and pulls his fingers from my mouth.

"We can't have that," I tell him, a smile on my face.

"No. We can't," he replies. "One day soon I'm gonna take this ass, baby, but today is not that day." His voice has dropped again, the gravelly tone even more commanding. "I'm going to release your hands. You will not move them. Understand?"

My shoulders ache but as much as I want to move them, and I do, because I want to know what would come after, I give in to him. "Yes."

He releases my wrists and true to my word I don't move, but when he pulls away from me, the emptiness creeps in. It threatens me, wrapping itself around my heart. It's barbed wire and it hurts, digging into a heart whose beat was starting to mean something. It's not clean, it's messy, and I can't move. I can't pull away with the jagged barbs holding me prisoner.

There's rustling behind me, and then fingers caress my spine, dragging down my body and wrapping around my wrists.

"Cassius." His name is a whimper. A plea. To hold me or to let me go?

Please don't let me go.

He drives his cock into me without warning. My heart swells, and even though the barbs dig deeper, the wire snaps, leaving me with scars. But scars fade, and hearts beat. And mine beats for him. For me. For this.

He pounds into me hard, my shoulders still aching from their position, but I don't care. His available hand snakes under my stomach, brushing against my clit. I moan in appreciation, and his fingers rub gently, skillfully.

When he finds the spot, I cry out, "Yes! Yes, Cassius!" He circles it quicker, flicks it harder, the river swells, the dam breaks and we're both swimming in my pleasure.

Cassius releases my wrists and grabs my hips, pulling me up slightly. He pushes and pulls me, chasing his own release. I shift my arms underneath me and push myself up. Cassius wraps what's left of my braid around his hand and pulls my head back, forcing my hips down.

His speed increases, and he fucks me, losing all control. My pussy clenches around his cock, desperate to give him what he needs.

When he finally comes, it's with a primal yell.

And at this moment, I know I'll never be the same.

Twenty-Seven

"What?" Ruby asks, when she catches me staring. She's sitting on the island counter with one of my T-shirts hanging off one shoulder. Struck by the normalcy, I step between her legs and press my lips to the bare skin.

"Isabella Diaz is alive and well and living in a suburb in Florida. She just got her GED and is going to the community college part-time while she works at Publix as a cashier."

Ruby's eyes widen and she opens her mouth to say something, but must change her mind because nothing comes out. Turning from her, I open the fridge, retrieving sandwich makings. Placing them next to her on the cutting board, I continue, "So, I knew shit was going down. The underworld always knows, right? The sex traders started acting shady, well, shadier than usual. I had Garrett look into it."

I offer her a shrug and then hold up a tomato in question. She nods.

"Anyway, we found out that they've been trafficking, but until Isabella, it had been all out of town dealings. Nothing local. So, Cranston's son? Obsessed with Isabella—a local girl from a poor family. Her dad got wind of it and used it to his advantage. He sold her to Cranston, using the guys in the trade as the dealer. Smart if you think about it, but also stupid. So very stupid."

I hold up the lettuce, and again she nods. "I'm really not picky. I like pretty much everything."

"Well, that makes it easy." I tear off layers of lettuce and spread mayo on four slices of bread. "G sees this, it's an anomaly, a chink in their armor. I've done and still do things in my life I'm not proud of. But there are also things I can't sit back and let happen."

"We have that in common..." she tilts her head, pulling her upper lip into her mouth in thought, "to an extent." She spears a pickle with the fork and pops it in her mouth.

"So, long story short, G and I came up with a plan. I hit Cranston's kid with my car. Paralyzing him was a perk, not necessarily my intention. I wanted him to suffer, but I wanted it to be by my hands. While he was in ICU, G worked his magic with Cranston's home security, and I took the girl right out from under Cranston's nose. I was rough with her, shoved her in the trunk. It had to look real because I didn't want them looking for her. It was better if they didn't. But it didn't matter because the footage was scrubbed, except for that piece your friend dug up. Still not sure how she found that one."

I cut both sandwiches in half and slide one toward her. Ruby bites into it with an appreciative moan. After last night, and then this morning, I figured she must be famished. I fill two glasses with water and offer her one.

The cold is refreshing, and I take several gulps before putting mine back down.

She drains the glass and takes another bite of her sandwich. She uses a hand to cover her mouth, talking through the bite. "So, the younger Cranston, Junior, he's paralyzed. I knew that." She swallows. "But what happened to Senior?"

"Like I said, I killed him." I finish half of my sandwich and wash it down with more water. "I thought he hired you to kill me. He's the only person I can think of because nobody that owes me money has the money to pay you. I can only assume that your price ... it must be high."

Ruby nods again, eyes wide with vigor. "Cassius, I honestly don't know who hired me. It's anonymous and Rowan has dug as deep as she can and has found nothing. Nada. Not a single trace of where the hit came from. And even if it was him, the hit doesn't go away. It's not like it disappears off the Reds' radar just because he's dead."

"Even if it wasn't him. He was a piece of shit that somebody should have killed a long time ago. Will you tell me about the Reds?"

"Only if I can soak in your tub while I do." Her eyes drop sheepishly. "I'm a little sore."

I am such an ass. Fuck.

"Baby, I am so sorry. I just, I ... I thought you'd be

hungry and my stomach and fuck. Of course, you can take a bath."

"Oh, I was starving, and I'm not sore the way you're thinking. I think my muscles and joints are sore from killing a half dozen, actually no, I think it was nine. Nine people last night, and then some asshole had my shoulders in a position they aren't used to."

I groan, and Ruby laughs. "That sore, it's a good sore. It just sucks that it's in combination with my other aches right now."

There are so many layers to this woman that I want to discover. I want to climb between each one and settle there. I want to know all the things that will make her laugh. I want to know her favorite song and if she can hold a tune. I want to know her best memory. And her worst. I want to know the deepest darkest parts of her, the ones that no one else gets to see. The ones she struggles to carry alone. I want to help her carry them.

I check my phone again, but there are no new texts, no missed calls. I didn't want to come to the club tonight. I tried everything I could to get out of it, especially after what she told me about the Reds. None of it sits well with me, and I want Garrett to look into it, but every time I open my mouth to ask him, I see Ruby's face. The one that's hurt and confused about the people who took care of her but in their own way destroyed her. It's clear that she's still trying to work everything out, and all I can do is be there when she does.

In the end, she convinced me it was safer this way, for both of us. Things have shifted between us, and more than anything, I want to go back home and curl up with her. But we have to keep up appearances. Publicly we need to hate each other for the Reds' sake at least. But it doesn't stop me from looking at my phone, anticipating a text that will probably never come.

"Cass." Garrett slams his glass on the table. "Are you going to tell me what the fuck is up with you or are you going to sit there moping all fucking night? The night is young and there is fresh ass on that floor."

"It's nothing," I tell him, averting my gaze. "Club shit, game shit, you know the drill." The lie tastes bitter, and I take a sip of my drink. I don't lie to my best friend. Ever. I have only ever lied by omission once in all our years of friendship, and it cost him. But this entire situation is bigger than anything we have ever been up against, and I can't risk him. Besides her, he's the only person I think I've ever truly cared about.

Garrett leans back in the booth and eyes me over the top of his glass. "Are we just going to pretend like I believe that?"

I say nothing, there's nothing to say.

He stands. "Well, I'm gonna go find some pussy while you," he waves a hand over me, "figure all this shit out. Let me know when you want some help." He walks down the steps and onto the dance floor, where he disappears.

My phone pings with a text.

Unknown number: You're not acting like yourself.

The text causes my heart to go into overdrive. How is this happening?

Unknown number: You normally make the rounds. You need to do that.

Normally I find a willing participant and go to my office.

Unknown number is typing…

Unknown number is typing…

Unknown number is typing…

I know you like to watch.

Radio silence. This is her right? Who the fuck else would it be? I stand and remove myself from the booth, casting my eyes around the club.

My phone pings.

Unknown number: No office booty call.

Unknown number: Unless it is me…

We can do that again. Maybe without so much blood next time

Unknown number: Is it the risk? Or the pain?

It's you.

Unknown number: Go dance. You do that sometimes, right?

Do I have to?

Unknown number: Appearances.

Putting my phone in my pocket, I blow my breath out slowly, audibly. This is the fucking last thing I want to be doing right now. Poker face, Cassius. Poker face. I walk down the steps and nod to the security guard at the VIP entrance. He nods back in response and takes out his phone to text the rest of the security team, letting them know I'll be on the floor.

The dance floor is busy, and it fucking smells—alcohol,

perfume, cologne, and body odor. They all hover like a storm cloud waiting to hit you in the face. Sweaty bodies surround me. I wade through them, narrowly avoiding having my junk grabbed by some woman wearing a veil and a sash that says BRIDE. I hate bachelorette parties, and I'm not saying that bachelor parties are any better, but bachelorette parties are loud and messy, and the women are always leaking makeup down their faces because someone is always crying.

I find a small group of women dancing together and slowly work my way between them. Gliding my hand over the small of one back, I flash a one-sided smirk at another. I'm greeted with smiles and grinding hips as I try to pretend this is where I want to be. A blonde woman grinds on one of my legs, trailing a finger down my chest. Her friend lingers for a minute and then moves behind me, grinding on my ass. I move my body with theirs. Normally this is where I would whisk one away, but I won't because all I can think about is getting home to Ember. Ember in my T-shirt. Ember in my bed. Ember on my dick.

Ember.

My watch vibrates with an incoming text.

Unknown number: ABORT.

Thank God. Extracting myself from the girls, I feign disappointment, gesturing that I have to go. Turning around, I come face to face with a ghost. She smiles and turns, pushing between groups of people and disappearing deeper into the dance floor. My feet are rooted where I stand. The bodies around me move in hyper-time while I'm in slow motion. Everything around me blurs.

Hannah.

But that's impossible. Hannah has been dead for twelve years.

Garrett stumbles into my line of sight, his face is white, his eyes wide.

He saw her too. He's no longer the twenty-eight-year-old tech genius, but the broken sixteen-year-old boy of his past. His face twists with anguish. His pupils dilate. I need to get him out of here. Fuck. I don't know who the fuck that was, but there's no way. *No fucking way.*

I grab Garrett by the arm and pull him from the dance floor, shoving bodies as I go. He moves like he's wading through sand, slow and heavy. I motion to one of the bouncers for help. Together we help him up the stairs. I can't wait for him to gain proper movement of his legs again. We need to figure out what the fuck just happened.

We deposit him on the couch and the bouncer leaves, the door locking behind him.

"G," I plead. "Tell me what you saw."

His eyes skate across the room until they finally land on me.

"Cass, she..." But he doesn't finish his sentence, instead he covers his mouth with his hand and runs to the bathroom behind me. He chokes and spurts, but nothing comes out. When the dry heaving stops, I speak.

"She's dead, Garrett. We saw her body."

"But Cass, her dad. He could have—"

"No, he couldn't. She's dead."

Realization dawns on both of us, but Garrett is the first one to say it out loud. "It was a closed casket."

175

"But there was no pulse." I pace. "And all that blood."

Garrett slides to the floor, leaning against the vanity.

"So much blood," he says.

Sirens go off in my head, and I call the unknown number. My single lie of omission has come to haunt me.

She answers on the first ring.

"It's Hannah," I say, not letting Ruby speak. "She's the person who hired you."

"Who is Hannah, Cassius?" Her voice is clipped, her words sharp.

"A fucking ghost."

Twenty-Eight

I am pacing in the foyer when Cassius walks in the door with Garrett behind him.

They're both pale, but while Garrett looks as though he might fall, Cassius looks like an addict, jittery and anxious. His eyes don't meet mine; they flit around the room without focus, which is unusual and unnerving. He always looks at me, even on the brink of death.

The air is thick with silence as I wait for him to say something, anything. Instead, he makes his way to the bar in the kitchen and grabs a bottle of tequila. He doesn't pour a glass or a shot. No, Cassius lifts the bottle to his lips and drinks.

In my hand, my phone rings, breaking up the fog that

chokes us. I blow out my breath and slide the green button over to answer it.

Here we fucking go.

"Rubes, I didn't miss anything, I promise. I don't know who she is," Rowan says before I can say hello.

I shift my eyes to Cassius, who squeezes his gray eyes shut, and when he opens them, they are glazed, vapid. He takes another sip of the tequila, his knuckles white from gripping the bottle, and then slams the bottle on the counter.

"Rowan, perfect timing." I prop my phone up on the kitchen counter so she can see all of us.

Putting my hands on my hips, I look pointedly at Cassius, who is now leaning on his elbows on the island, his chin in his hands. "One of you better start talking. Who is Hannah?"

Cassius shifts his gaze first to Rowan, then to me, and finally to Garrett, settling there.

"She's supposed to be dead," he says.

"She is dead," Garrett adds.

"But it was a closed casket."

"Dead or not dead, I need facts fellas," Rowan commands from the screen, "because Cassius, none of my research even mentioned a Hannah."

Garrett cracks his knuckles. "It doesn't make sense, Cass. If she was alive, she would have contacted me. Right? I mean, I loved her, and she loved me. We loved each other. Fuck, I still love her. I always have."

"Facts," Rowan yells. Has she ever yelled before? I rack my brain and can't think of a single time. "Stick to the facts."

Cassius straightens to standing and drags his hand over

his face in defeat or frustration, I can't tell. "Her name was ... is Hannah Flemming. When we were teenagers, she and Garrett were in love."

"There is no Hannah Flemming in my research," Rowan says matter-of-factly.

"Because what you're seeing is made up." Garrett moves closer to the tablet. "You're good, I'll give you that, but apparently not that good."

"We grew up in New Mexico, close to the border," Cassius says. "In a city called Echolls."

Rowan bites the inside of her cheek, the clacking of the keyboard in front of her the only indication she heard any of what they said. How could she have possibly missed this?

"We grew up in the Row." Cassius meets my eyes. "I didn't lie about that. We grew up and got out of some really shit situations."

"Hannah," Garrett winces as if only saying her name causes him physical pain. "She was good. Too good for me, and her dad let everyone know it."

"Got it." Rowan interrupts. "According to this article, Hannah got on the city bus and was later found on the front porch of a house, raped and murdered," she fills us all in, her fingers still typing a mile a minute.

"His house," Garrett says, gesturing to Cassius.

"They arrested a couple teens for it, but no charges were ever made," Rowan says from the screen.

"Us," Cassius says.

"You're Christopher Cruz and Gavin Sharp?" Rowan asks.

The men nod. "Our names were everywhere." Garrett

explains, "It took a lot of time and a lot of money for us to fabricate new identities, because we couldn't just change our names. We needed foolproof backgrounds. Apparently, it worked."

"Are we forgetting the fact that she's dead?" Rowan asks. "I am staring at her obituary. Rubes, I'm sending it to your phone now."

"So, it was a closed casket?" I ask, repeating what they said earlier, while I wait for the obituary to come through. "But Cassius, why would she want you dead? None of this makes sense."

"She was at the club," Garrett answers. "She's alive." He leans back in his stool, color coming back into his cheeks. His bright eyes close briefly before opening again. His gaze flits between his best friend, the assassin, and the girl on my phone. He stands abruptly, knocking the stool over.

Cassius moves to the other side of the island.

"She," Garrett points at me and then Cassius, his hand shaking, the vein in his forehead prominent. "She's right, what did you do? Why the fuck does Hannah want you dead?" He picks the bottle of tequila up off the counter and throws it on the floor next to Cassius. Glass skitters across the floor and what was left of the tequila pools at Cassius' feet.

"G." Cassius' shoulders drop. "I'm sorry, I never wanted it to go that far. I never, I never thought they would follow through."

"Who would follow through? With what?" Garrett raises his voice, stepping into Cassius' personal space. He's not as big as Cassius, but the fear and anger radiating off him makes him a threat. Cassius shrinks back as regret takes over his features.

"It's all my fault." Cassius takes a step back from Garrett, broken glass crunching beneath his feet, and grips the back of his neck with his hand. "I hustled the wrong people."

"What the fuck are you talking about?"

"You were so wrapped up in Hannah, and I was bored, man." Cassius winces at his own admission, shrinking smaller with every word. "I played cards with some people, men in suits. I don't fucking know who they were, but I knew they were important. Their suits, G, they cost more than anything we owned."

Garrett doesn't move. His fists clench at his sides and the vein in his neck throbs, but his feet remain planted.

"The guy Neil that was hanging around my mom at the time, you remember him? He told me where I could find their game. So, I went. And I played. I lost the first few rounds, on purpose, of course. And then I won, and I kept fucking winning. I could taste it, G. Freedom. For both of us."

"What the actual fuck," Garrett spits. "What does this have to do with Hannah?"

"The next day, they must have put two and two together and went after Neil. Neil gave me up. Told them I was a cheat. They pounded down the fucking door, held a fucking gun to my head, and told me I had twenty-four hours to give the money back, or they'd kill my girl. I didn't have a girl, so it didn't matter to me."

Cassius pauses. His Adam's apple bobs as he swallows. "When we found Hannah, I realized that Neil must have thought she was mine because the two of us hung at the house a lot while we waited for you to get out of school. He must have thought..." He pinches his eyes closed and takes a deep breath. "He must have told them about Hannah. It's the only thing I can think of." He looks at Garrett. "I'm so sorry G."

"You piece of fucking shit." Garrett shoves Cassius, "How could you keep this from me?"

"I thought you would blame me, and you should. I never should have played with them in the first place."

Garrett steps back, turning away from Cassius. It happens in a flash, one second, he's walking away and the next the two are on the ground, Garrett with the upper hand but only because Cassius is still. He takes the beating as his penance, as if living with the knowledge has not been enough.

"I should fucking kill you myself!" Garrett is purple with rage; his veins threaten to burst with every hit he throws at Cassius. "You were supposed to be my best friend."

"I am," Cassius gurgles, blood sputtering from lips. "I didn't know G, I swear."

"Rubes, stop them. I need facts," Rowan yells from her screen.

I pull a blade from my waistband and touch the cold steel to Garrett's throat.

"Enough," I say. "We have work to do." Using my blade, I point to the stools and then to the men. "Sit. Now."

I know that my feelings for Cassius should make me feel sympathetic to his injuries, but instead I find myself turned on. I want to drag my tongue over the cut on his lip, to feel the roughness beneath my touch. I wonder if he would lay there and take it while I did unspeakable things to him.

"Did the men ever come back looking for the money?" I ask.

Cassius shakes his head. "No. I kept expecting them to,

but they never did."

"While you two were acting like children," Rowan says, "I've been going through her obituary line by line looking for anything that could help us. The first thing that's odd is that there isn't a picture, and even a thorough search of her doesn't bring one up."

"Her dad was into some shit, international business shit," Garrett supplies. "He was very private and forced the girls to be private too."

"After they didn't come back for the money, I started to wonder if the suits knew her dad, and realized they fucked up," Cassius offers a shrug. "Or maybe it was on purpose, and their play with me was just a cover."

"I'll look into it. But here's the other thing," Rowan continues, "the obit is clean. Like, it says that Hannah Flemming died, but services were for close family only and doesn't mention any of them by name."

"If it was a closed service, how do the two of you know it was a closed casket?" I ask.

"We blackmailed the funeral director to let us in before the family," Cassius answers.

"He was having an affair with his wife's sister," Garrett says. "It was child's play."

"You said girls." Rowan backtracks.

I throw Cassius a dish towel from the drawer, and he uses it to wipe the blood from his face. His eye is puffy, and I think his nose needs to be reset. Again.

"Hannah had... has? A sister," Cassius offers. "I don't remember her name, though."

"Sophie," Garrett supplies. "She and Hannah were like

eight or nine years apart."

The three of us stare at the phone, the rhythmic tapping of Rowan's keyboard the only noise in the room.

"She doesn't exist. How is that possible?" Rowan lets out a frustrated groan. "And why are there no fucking pictures? Rubes, I'm going to need a little time to get into the county database, see if I can pull up the case file on Hannah."

Garrett digs into his pocket, pulling out his wallet. "I have a picture. Of Hannah, I mean, but I don't know how much good it will do. It's pretty beat up."

"And you just thought of this now? I could have been running facial recognition this entire fucking time." Rowan bobs her head forward. "And you call yourself a genius."

"Excuse me if I'm rattled after the ghost of the only girl I've ever loved made a fucking appearance tonight," Garrett bites back. "And the guy who's supposed to be a brother, is the fucking reason why." He removes a photo strip from his wallet and slides it across the counter to me without looking at it. It's from a photo booth. The kind where two teenagers kiss and laugh.

Four black and white pictures. In them, the man in front of me is no more than a child. There are deep creases across his features, where the strip has been folded and unfolded over the years. Some of the finish has rubbed off in places, evidence of time gone by. He never once looks at the camera, his eyes stay firmly planted only on the girl. It makes me think that he sees her through the torn edges, through the creases. He folds and unfolds, and opens out of habit, to feel close to her, not because he forgets. He must see her every time he closes his eyes. "Is this all you have?" I ask Garrett.

He nods and reaches for it, but instead of handing it back to him, I snap a photo and text it to Rowan.

"Work your magic with that, Row."

A ping sounds and she stretches her arms out, cracks her knuckles, then moves her head side to side as if preparing for a fight. Always the theatrics. We watch as she takes in the photo. Her face pales, and her features go slack.

"Rubes," her voice is barely a whisper. "This is a problem." She puts a finger to her lips and looks over her shoulder like someone might be standing behind her. "I'll call you back," she says, and the screen goes black.

TWENTY-NINE

Rowan doesn't call back. The hours pass slowly, each tick of the clock louder than the last. On the bedside table, Ruby's phone sits quiet and dark except for the blinking light indicating it being charged.

"Something is wrong," I say for the twentieth time.

Ruby tears her eyes from the ceiling to look at me. "Nothing is wrong, she's being careful. Clearly, she saw something in those photos that I didn't. She'll call when she can."

"But what if she doesn't?"

She puts her phone down. "She will."

She turns toward me, her red hair splayed across the pillow in swirls of garnet. Her ivory skin is almost iridescent in the moonlight. The tip of her finger grazes the scab on my lip, then moves to my swollen eye. Gently, I pull the sheet down and away from her breasts. They spill out, free from the confines of fabric. I cup one in my hand, feeling the fullness of it. The softness.

I'm not sure how someone so hard and sharp can be so soft and delicate. I brush my thumb over her nipple and her entire body stills. I pull it into my mouth, grazing the sensitive spot with my teeth. Her hands find my hair, her fingers soft and light as they tangle in it.

I push her gently to her back and climb on top of her. My tongue trails up her breast and along her collarbone, planting feather-like kisses that make her tense beneath my lips.

"Cassius, what about," she whispers.

"Shh," I murmur against her neck, cutting off her protests. I take her earlobe between my teeth, tugging it just hard enough to make her moan.

"Right now, it's just you and me," I whisper into her ear. "And the only thing I want to do right now is worship my queen."

I kiss her softly, teasing her tongue with my own. "I'm going to find every spot that makes you whimper, every place that makes you tense beneath my touch." I kiss her again. "I'm going to make you tremble with need and burn with desire."

I am awarded with a shiver, and it feels like an eruption. Like life exploding at my fingertips.

Our eyes meet, and I feel her in the deepest parts of me, navigating all my broken parts. But instead of trying to fix me, instead of trying to glue the shattered parts of me back together, she settles in and fills the empty spaces, making me whole.

My lips crash into hers, swallowing the moment, committing it to memory. Her tongue touches mine, tentative and sweet. I slide mine across hers, our mouths saying everything without saying anything at all. Her fingers skate across my naked back, and now I am the one who shivers.

I trace her jawline with my lips, my hands exploring the rest of her. They glide down her body, and my mouth follows. I trace her nipples with my tongue and look up at her as I gently blow on them. Goosebumps erupt over her body, and I move my face to the valley between her breasts, my hands a little rougher as I bite the inside of one.

Ruby squirms beneath me, her fingers making their own discoveries as they try to make their way between my legs.

I pull her arms up and hold her wrists over her head, and she traps her bottom lip between her teeth.

I drop my jaw and look at her expectantly. She sighs, but when I remove my hand from her wrists, she leaves them there.

I kiss her scars, cherishing each one, wishing I could release her from the things that haunt her. There are so many that I can't even comprehend how many demons she battles on a daily basis. I pay special attention to the one that starts under her left breast and continues across the span of her torso to her right hip. Someday, I'll ask her about that one.

I move down her body, savoring the way she sucks in a breath when I spread her legs and climb between her thighs. Her skin tastes sweet on my tongue as I skim it down one leg before making my way back up to her inner thigh. I bring the taut skin there into my mouth, and she inhales sharply. I suck lightly at first and then harder, marking her as my own. Her legs stiffen in anticipation, but her hands remain where I put them.

I twirl the tip of my tongue near her center and back along her inner thighs, barely touching her. Her breaths are quick and shallow as her body clenches, her legs tightening around me.

I lift my head to look at her, her eyes are squeezed closed, and her knuckles are white against the headboard.

"Baby, breathe," I coax. Her eyes open to glare at me, clouded and sinister. "This will be so much better if you relax." I dip my head back down and slide my tongue along her slit, she shudders. "I promise."

I tease her with my tongue, getting close to, but never touching her clit. Her breaths get deeper, and I reward her with a flick to her sensitive nub.

"Cassius," she moans, her voice breathy and dripping with need.

I slip a finger into her pussy and a gasp escapes her lips. Slowly I finger fuck her while using my tongue to play with her clit. Frustration coats every sound she makes, but I take my time because when I finally let her orgasm, it's going to be an explosion of pleasure.

I add a second finger, and she shifts her hips up to meet me. Abandoning her clit, I glide my tongue to join my fingers, sucking softly on her folds.

"Oh my God," she utters between clenched teeth.

"Not God." My voice is muffled by her pussy, and I know the vibrations are killing her when her thighs trap my head in a death grip. "Who's your king, baby?" I ask her, pausing all my movements while I wait for her to answer.

She reaches for me, and I follow her pull back up her body.

Ruby takes my face in her hands, hands that have taken the last breath of so many. Hands that have been covered in blood more often than they've probably been clean. But it doesn't matter, none of that matters, because I trust her with my life.

"You, Cassius." She pulls my face to hers, her lips claiming my own.

We fit together, our bodies in sync as I line my cock up with her entrance. She tugs on my bottom lip, and I don't hesitate any longer. I enter her slowly, and when I'm buried to the hilt, she smiles. I take my time, gliding in and out of her, planting soft kisses on her lips and down her neck. She whimpers a little when I get to the spot behind her ear, and I increase my speed slightly. Leaning back, I lift one of her legs to rest on my shoulder, changing the way my cock hits her inside to find the spot that will undo her.

Using one hand to hold me up, I use my free hand to rub her clit, starting slow and then increasing the speed to match my thrusts. Her breaths are heavier, quicker, her pussy clenches around my cock with every thrust, and I know she's close.

Sliding her leg to my other shoulder, I twist her body and let my hips slap against her ass. Her body starts to tremble, so I increase the momentum. The muscles in her ass clench, her legs quake and she covers my cock with her pleasure. Her juices drip down me as I drive into her, seeking my own release.

"You're mine, Cassius, my king." Her voice is the catalyst to my undoing, and I pull out, fisting my cock and pumping my seed across her body.

THIRTY

W hen Cassius has thoroughly cleansed me of his semen, he lies on his back and pulls me into his side. My head rests on his chest, and I count his heartbeats.

Thud. One.

Thud. Two.

Thud. Three.

The world is silent except for the pounding in his chest.

Thud. Four.

Thud. Five.

I push closer to him, wanting our two bodies to become one.

Thud. Thud. Thud.

I lose count when his heartbeat speeds. I feel him open

his mouth to say something, but he closes it again before any words come out.

I'm glad he doesn't say it. He doesn't need to. I know because I feel it too. Our bodies, our souls, the shattered pieces of us, they're mixed together now, and I no longer know which pieces are mine and which are his.

I sigh into him, calm flooding my body.

In my peripheral, the screen of my phone flashes and then it rings with an incoming video call. We both startle at the intrusion, the moment lost.

I press the button to accept the call, and Rowan appears on the screen. Wherever she is, it's dark, the only light coming from the screen, turning her face pale and sullen.

"Rubes," she starts, but I interrupt her.

"Where are you, Row?"

She swallows. "In my closet, but listen, it doesn't matter where I am, it's the only place I can talk about this. We have a major problem. You don't recognize Hannah, do you?"

I shake my head and look at Cassius, who shrugs. "I don't know why you would," he says.

"Rubes, it's Rawlings."

Rawlings? That doesn't make sense.

"Hannah is Rawlings?" I ask.

"Not quite, now listen. I don't have long. Someone is going to discover this soon enough, and shit is going to hit the fan."

"Row, I—"

"Not. Now. Rubes. Just listen. I can't talk. It's not safe. I'm sending you an encrypted file. Give it to Garrett, he'll know what to do. I gotta go."

Her eyes shift to something off camera, and the call ends. My phone falls on the bed between me and Cassius before vibrating, an email notification appearing at the top of the screen. I freeze, a statue of uncertainty. Rowan looked terrified, on edge even. Is someone after her or, worse, hurting her?

"Here," Cassius says, interrupting my free fall into my intrusive thoughts. He pulls on the pants he discarded earlier and throws me his shirt. I step into my panties and slide my arms into its soft sleeves. I miss a button in my rush for answers but don't bother to fix it. There's no time for that, not now.

Cassius lets out a long breath, and when I look up at him, I'm taken aback by the expression I see there. A small smile is spread across his face, but there's no hunger in it like I expect to see. Instead, his smile is warm and peaceful. It heats my insides like a crackling fire on a snowy winter night. Comfortable and safe.

Fires though, can't always be contained and as my heart beats for Cassius, it pours gasoline on the flames that lick at my thoughts. It engulfs my soul, smothering any chance of self-preservation. My life no longer exists without Cassius. I will destroy anyone who threatens him. I will burn this world to the ground until it is nothing but ash and Ember.

Everything is so confusing, and it's all blending together, tangling in knots that I can't untie. Worry for Rowan, the truth about my feelings for Cassius, suddenly it all feels like too much. My heart beats faster, erratic, like it might pound right out of my chest. My breath quickens, and I gasp, my lungs desperate for air. Blinking back tears, I swallow, trying to swallow down the feelings, to push them down to where they used to live.

Strong protective arms surround me, pulling me close.

Cassius puts a finger under my chin, lifting my face to look at him, and then crushes his lips to mine. His kiss silences the noise and douses the flame. I never want to move. I want to live right here, forever in his arms. Safe in the quiet, getting lost in his kiss.

When he finally pulls away, he does it slowly, like it's painful to separate himself from me. His eyes narrow at me in concern before he pulls me tighter to him, the side of my face snug against his bare chest. His lips press tenderly into my hair.

"I got you Ember," he whispers, his voice barely a breath. "I got you."

Ember.

THIRTY-ONE

"This is fucked," Garrett grits his teeth and stands, his hands raised out in front of him. "I can't do this, man."

Photos of Hannah are scattered on the computer screen. Ruby takes the vacant seat Garrett left at my desk and enlarges each crime scene photo one by one. Unlike Garrett, I can't bring myself to look away. Each photo is worse than the one before it. Numbered tags mark blood splatters and pieces of clothing. A shoe print, a knife, a woman's flip-flop, a young woman's lifeless body. There's a photo of her bottom half, in it her legs are bent at odd angles, the joints rigid. She sits in a dark red pool, her skirt pushed up on her hips. In the last photo, her empty eyes stare back at us, daring us to look away.

Her arms are stretched above her head, her wrists secured with a strip of fabric to the post behind her. A split gold chain dangles between angry red lines painted on her neck and chest.

"They used her underwear," I tell Ruby, pointing to Hannah's wrists. "And that chain, it had a charm on it. A heart made of cubic zirconia, G got for her. I don't know why the suits would have taken it, maybe they thought it would throw suspicion?" Ruby nods, continuing her study of the photos. Across the room, Garrett gets sick in the trash can.

I'm not sure what she expects to find in the photos that will help us, but she studies them, committing them to memory. Each blood drop, every scratch, all the purple bruises. I'm grateful when she finally closes all the photos and reopens the folder Rowan sent.

I motion to Garrett and watch as he rolls the defeat off his back before joining me behind Ruby.

"Hannah is dead. Those pictures have not been doctored." Ruby is tactless. I wince and then look over at Garrett, who may or may not get sick again. Before he does, she continues, "Which means that Rowan is correct, and the woman you saw was not Hannah."

Ruby opens the only other file in the folder. A photo of an adult Hannah fills the screen.

"Fuck," Garrett says at the same time I ask, "How?"

"This is Rawlings."

"I think I'm gonna be sick again," Garrett mumbles, reaching for the trash can.

"Who the fuck is Rawlings?" I demand.

"Sophie," Ruby answers in her monotone voice as she

opens the next file.

"So, where the fuck is she and why are we not moving?" I open the desk drawer and retrieve my Smith and Wesson. Removing the magazine, I confirm that it's loaded and slip it back into place. The familiar sound like music to my ears. I look at Garrett, who hasn't moved, but instead just stares at the computer screen, his eyes darting back and forth taking in what he sees there.

Ruby looks up at me, her lips pulled in a straight line, her jaw set.

"Cassius, I know that the whole barge in and take care of business tactic is your style, but that's not how to handle this. We're talking about the Reds. We need to know what we're getting into before," she gestures at the gun in my hand, "we go in guns blazing."

"I will not be the pawn in this bitch's twisted game. She dies."

Ruby stands and places her hand on my cheek. "Cassius Cross has never been a pawn in anyone's game, and if she doesn't see that, perhaps she should be playing a different one."

"She dies," I repeat.

Her lips turn up, a devious smirk plays on her face. "She dies slowly."

Ruby's eyes grow dark, lustful. I pull her to me, pressing my lips with force against hers. Her nails rake the back of my neck, and I can feel her body writhe against mine.

This woman may no longer want to kill me, but she will be the end of me.

"If you two are done," Garrett clears his throat. "Rowan

did some serious digging here. And Ruby," he looks pointedly at her, "you're gonna have to fill in some blanks."

"Talk us through it, G," I tell him, and Ruby and I gather behind him.

"Okay, so it looks like Rowan dug into Rawling's background. She was recruited by your European chapter according to this docket here."

"That I know. We have chapters all over the world. Rawlings came to us about five years ago now, I think."

"September is five years, yeah. So anyway, I think we need to start from the beginning. The basics though are this, Hannah's dad killed himself not long after Hannah was killed, and her mom remarried six months later. Her new beau adopted Sophie and from what I can gather from Rowan's files he was a real fucking gem. They legally changed not only her last name, but also her first name. So, Sophie Flemming became Francesca Juarez after this jack-off's mother. How fucked up is that? Don't answer that, let me finish. Dude was an asshole, as you can already tell."

"Is there a picture of him?" I interrupt.

Garrett pulls up a picture, and it's my turn to be sick. "That's one of the suits."

"You sure?" Garrett shoots me a pained look. "It's been twelve years."

"Their faces have been etched in my brain for every last one."

"So, this cocksucker, he was a shithead. There are several reports of abuse, physical and sexual. But we all know money in the right hands will make all that go away. Except, her mom witnessed the last incident and blamed Francesca for making advances. Mommy dearest shipped her off to prep school the next day. Francesca was kicked out of prep school after prep school for organizing fighting rings until five years ago."

"When she was recruited by the Reds," Ruby finishes.

"Whatever the fuck that is," Garrett flaps his hand in the air, feigning indifference.

"In short, we're a league of assassins who recruit girls or women out of dangerous situations and train them to be contract killers."

Garrett spins in the chair and levels Ember with eyes that might possibly seal his own fate.

"How old were you?"

"Eight."

Garrett nods, eyes wide. "They're supposed to protect us."

They're supposed to protect us, but they didn't. Have we become what we are because of our parents? Or in spite of them? I know the answer, it's neither. We became what we are because we didn't have a choice. We became what we are to survive. And now, now, we thrive on the violence it takes to do so. It jumpstarts our hearts and pumps our blood through our veins.

"Fuck them," I growl and look from G to Ruby and back again. I gesture to the three of us. "We survived. We fucking won."

"Life is not a game, Cass." Garrett whispers, looking at the screen again.

Ember meets my gaze, and I know without looking in a mirror that my smile matches hers. We both know life is a game, and we're about to flip the fucking board.

THIRTY-TWO

I have never understood what people mean when they say home is not a place. Until now. The house is stagnant when I enter, stale with routine. It feels almost clinical, like I'm not supposed to be here. And I suppose I'm not. Not anymore.

My feet tread lightly over the wooden floors, and I step over the boards that I know will creak. Waking the rest of the house up right now would not be in my best interest. I need to go on as if my heart has not been bleeding out for hours while Cassius slept next to me. Sleep never came for me because I know what he doesn't. I know that choices are not something I have. I signed away my right to choices when I became Ruby.

I unlock and open the door to my suite. Entering the room, I half expect Rowan to be curled up in here, but it's empty. Cold. Lifeless.

Carefully, quietly, I close the door behind me, locking it tight. Leaning with my back against the door, I pull out my phone to reread Rowan's text. It came a few hours ago, while Cassius slept, and I watched. He was so peaceful in his slumber, his breath stealing mine as we faced each other on the pillows. I take a deep breath, clearing my lungs, and unlock my phone.

Rowan: OK! High @ 7am Sry

A last-minute high court meeting can only mean one thing. It's about me, about Cassius. I rub my temples and look at the time on my phone. 5:17. That gives me just under two hours to prepare. I wish Rowan were here right now; she could help. But based on the last time I saw her on our video call, I imagine whatever she's up to is dangerous for either her or someone else, which I don't know.

I don't know a lot of things lately, and it is beginning to fuck with my head. What I once thought was up is now down, and what was once a way of life I wanted seems so out of place.

What I do know for certain? There's only one way out of this.

I use the time while everyone is still waking from their slumber to get myself ready— physically and mentally. I wash away the last few days, cleansing myself of Cassius. Ridding myself of his scent, of his touch. I scrub at the memories, the ones where he held me close. The ones where I fought him and he did not fight back, but instead brought me down to solid ground. The ground where I found the footing I thought I'd lost. The ground that seemed so far away but now sits sturdy beneath me.

A text comes through on my burner, but I delete it without reading it. I know it's Cassius, who just woke up and found his bed empty. I knew it would come. I could have ditched the phone on my ride home. I could have run over it with my bike. I could have stomped on it. But it was a test I forced upon myself instead. One that, apparently, I passed.

Which is good because *Cassius must die.*

THIRTY-THREE

Walking into the meeting space feels like walking into a hall of mirrors. Eyes are everywhere, taking in every move I make. The five other high queens stare at me from a monitor on the wall as I take my seat. Their faces are like stone, the only thing soft about them are the wrinkles that the Ruby from Europe has at the corners of her eyes.

She's the first of us to show any signs of aging. Rubys do not grow old. They disappear. They die. They get replaced. In the end, we are all replaced one way or another. I have spent my life as Ruby thinking I was invincible, but as I look around at the others, I know the truth. We're all replaceable.

I make eye contact with the latest replacement Ruby from Africa. Her eyes are cold and deep. Two black holes pull me into their abyss. Her dark skin is flawless like silk and although she's the youngest, the greenest of all of us, it's her that makes me the most uneasy. As if she reads my mind, she smiles. Her white teeth like that of a shark, gleaming and hungry.

My lips turn up in my own smile, because as much as I understand that I'm replaceable, I also know that I'm the one they should all be afraid of. I'm the one that hunts at night, the one with feet as silent as a ghost. I'm the Ruby the world should fear.

"Now that we're all here," Asia's Ruby commands our attention in her perfect English, "let us discuss why we're interrupting our busy schedules. Plead your case, North America."

"There is nothing to plead, ladies," I say, the words floating off my tongue. "To be quite honest, I'm not sure why this meeting has even been called. I am working a mark and you interrupted it."

The silence in the room is deafening. Did they really expect me to come in here and show my hand? Amateurs. All of them.

"This job is taking longer than usual," I continue, "because I have had to spend time vetting it due to where the order came from. Did you know it came from within the Reds?" I narrow my eyes at each of them in turn, daring them to contradict me. "And forgive me if I'm incorrect, but personal vendettas are not part of my job description, or yours for that matter. Each Red is to handle her own vendetta; however she deems fit. So how, ladies, did this get this far?"

"Rawlings submitted a formal request to me herself,"

Europe retorts, her wrinkles more prominent with each syllable. "As her original recruiter, and chapter liaison, that was protocol."

"Protocol?" I scoff. "To keep her true identity and the truth behind this mark from me? All that did was open me up to danger. Danger that could have been avoided had I been provided all the information."

Europe leans forward, the scowl on her face menacing, and I wonder if I've underestimated her. "Providing you or anyone with her true identity would have been dangerous. It would have made her a target. You must see who you're dealing with."

Understanding dawns on me. "You think he would have recognized her and gone after her?"

Europe nods. "Now, it has been brought to our attention that you have not been operating as a Red. That you have worked through all the steps and yet Mr. Cross lives and breathes. Why is that?"

South America hums in agreement, and I throw her a pointed glare.

"Mr. Cross has proven to be a formidable opponent. He has resources that rival our own, and in addition to that, he's a violent man. I have been careful. I have been weaving in and out of his periphery, and if I am being honest, Rawlings stunt the other night showing up at his club looking like Hannah, put him in a good place for me to take care of. He's spooked. His IT guy is spooked. Spooked people make stupid mistakes. Mistakes that will cost them their lives."

South America rolls her eyes. "You're lying."

"What reason could I possibly have to lie?" I counter.

"Mr. Cross will die; I promise you that."

"You have had every opportunity. You have recently been, ah, what do they call it? Ah sí, AWOL. And now you sit here and lie through your teeth. Where have you been?"

"I'm sure you know by now that my parents are dead."

"Your point?"

"After I killed them, I got dragged away for a recruitment about three hours from here. I stayed several days and would have stayed longer if not for this meeting."

"Where is the girl?"

"Enough," Europe raises her voice. "North America, you have been accused of consorting with your mark and are flirting dangerously with being charged with treason."

My heart pounds in my chest, but my face remains stoic. The face of a warrior, the face of someone with nothing to hide, nothing to lose. I raise an eyebrow of disbelief at Europe and then at the others.

"If you are looking for me to give you some kind of explanation, I will not because the accusations are exactly that. Accusations. Accusations with no basis whatsoever. And if you want to charge me with treason, you'll have to bring more to the table than your weak threats."

"Exhibit A," Australia responds, and a picture of me straddling Cassius on the hood of his car appears in the corner of the screen. "Is this not you?"

"It is, you know it is. And that knife at his throat? That's mine too." I smirk confidently.

"And this is you also? Please pay special attention to the time stamp in the corner."

It's a video clip of me in Cassius' shirt in his office last night. Garrett sitting at the desk, me and Cass standing behind him. My stomach drops to my knees and bile rises in my throat. Where the fuck did they get this? How do they have access to Cassius' cameras? Besides through Rowan, and I know she would never betray me. Ever. Right?

"Did you or did you not just tell us you were on a recruiting trip?" Africa sneers. "How could you be in two places at once?"

"I was on a recruiting trip, I stopped at Mr. Cross' for some last-minute recon before I came home early this morning."

"Have you ever done recon without a disguise prior to last night?" South America digs, her accent growing thicker to match the air in the room.

I clear my throat, commanding the women on the screens before me to listen. "As I said, Mr. Cross has proven to be quite the opponent. I have to earn his trust, and after last night I believe I have. Bleeding hearts make humans vulnerable, and with a mark like Mr. Cross, I need him that way. He bared his heart to me, and now he will bare his throat, gifting me an opening to drag my blade across it. I will bathe in his blood, as I have with all the others."

"Dios mío," South America mutters. "Why must you always paint such a picture?"

I smirk and shrug my shoulders. Game on bitch.

"He dies tonight," Asia says. "Enough games, enough waiting. We know you're the best, now fucking prove it or face our wrath."

A wicked grin plays at my lips. "Cassius Cross will die tonight."

The screens turn dark, leaving me alone to stew in the mess I've made. A mess of my own destruction. Cassius dies, and then Rawlings. When I have bled them both dry, Europe will hang like a pig in a slaughterhouse and one by one the queens will fall.

THIRTY-FOUR

I t's been eighteen hours without a word from her. Eighteen hours since she slipped away under the cover of night. Eighteen hours of unknown. G has been trying to track her with traffic cams, but so far has been unsuccessful. I refuse to believe she just left. That after everything, this is how it ends.

In front of me, the heavy bag sways from the force of my fist. Smears of blood litter the surface from my raw knuckles. My veins throb, my muscles cord with tension. Tension I thought I had felt the last of. Tension I thought I would never feel again.

I pound the bag, over and over. The thuds reverberate in my head, echoing my labored breathing.

"Jesus, how are you not keeled over yet?" Garrett asks

when he enters the gym.

I shoot him a glare and hit the bag again. The strip of duct tape running down the center rips, exposing the original tear. Exposing its scars, like Ruby's exposed mine. "You better fucking have something," I say through gritted teeth, hitting the bag again.

"They don't call her a ghost for nothing."

"You found her last time."

"Yeah," Garrett says sheepishly, "because she fucking let me. I'm telling you, man, she's gone."

"You're supposed to be the best."

"I am the best."

"Apparently fucking not."

"Fuck you, man, you realize this is all your fucking fault, right? You were the idiot? It's your fault that Hannah died. It's your fault that Sophie's life went to shit. Fuck, you'll be lucky if I don't fucking kill you myself."

"I deserve that," I admit.

"I don't even know how to look at you, Cass." Garrett drags his hand over his face. "Tell me this, the money you made off the suits? That's what we used to escape, right?"

I nod.

"Every bone in my body hates you right now. And you're lucky I'm terrified of your assassin girlfriend, or I probably would have killed you the other night. I know I just said Hannah's death was your fault, but I know it wasn't. You had no way of knowing. But Cass, you could have told me. We could have taken those suit fuckers and Neil out ten years ago. Who the fuck knows what other fucked up shit they've done since?"

He can spew whatever bullshit he wants, but Hannah's death is on me, and that's something I have to live with forever.

"Also," Garrett paces in front of me, "I kind of expected Ruby to kill you by now."

"She is not trying to kill me," I hesitate. "Anymore."

"Cass, she's fucking playing you. She's an assassin. The best assassin. The assassin that kills people like us just because she can."

I feel the bones crunch beneath my fist before I register what I've done. Blood gushes out of Garrett's nose, splattering the mat beneath our feet.

"Real friends tell you the truth," he says and then he spits blood at my feet before turning his back to me.

A buzzing noise fills the room and then stops.

Garrett turns to look at me, eyes wide. "Is that?" He gestures with his head to my phone.

I nod before picking my phone up off the bench. A single text flashes on the screen.

Unknown number: Midnight ride. Alone.

"What the fuck does that mean?" Garrett asks from behind me, reading over my shoulder.

"It means I've gotta go."

Garrett trails behind me as I leave the gym and head to my room to change. She wants to meet. What does this mean? Garrett's words haunt me, even though I don't want to believe them.

"Where are you going?"

"A place we've met before."

"You're not going to tell me where?"

"No."

"Why?"

"I don't want you to interfere. If she wanted to kill me, she would have already." But even as I say it, I check the mag of my 380 and chamber a round before putting it in its holster attached to my belt. "Besides," I continue, "you need to go have your nose reset."

Garrett exits my bathroom with a wet cloth, swiping at the blood on his face. "Eh." He shrugs. "I kind of thought the crooked nose thing was in. Chicks love a good story."

I smile because this is me and G. This is our story. Our truth. Our friendship. We have ups and downs and ebbs and flows, but at the end of the day, we're ride or die.

"You know I can just track the Impala, right?"

"But you're not going to unless you hear from me."

Garrett looks at me pointedly, waiting for me to continue.

"Or don't hear from me," I relent. "If you don't hear from me by 1 a.m., it means I'm probably bleeding out and you should kidnap a doctor to bring with you."

"Not funny."

"Wasn't trying to be."

THIRTY-FIVE

I kill the engine and climb out of the car. The full moon illuminates the sky, providing barely enough light for me to see the beautiful redhead standing outside the guardrail at the edge of the cliff. I expect her to turn as I approach, but she doesn't. She is a statue, a goddess of stone. A queen admiring her kingdom.

I hesitate to touch her, nervous that I'll startle her and consequently lose her to the terrain below. Instead, I come to a stop next to her and wait for her to acknowledge my presence.

Minutes pass, the silence so thick that I clear my throat in an attempt to rid myself of the ominous feeling. She releases a heavy sigh in response before turning and stepping over to the safe side of the guardrail. She drinks me in, hollowing out her cheeks in a way that makes my cock twitch.

"Rawlings or Sophie, whichever you'd like to call her, is the one who ordered the hit. She paid the price for you to die," she says, matter-of-factly.

"We knew that."

Ruby raises her eyebrows at me, a silent scolding. "Like any other court, we have laws. While she did not go outside of them, she most definitely bent them."

"So what happens now?"

"Reds do not retire, Cassius."

She takes an intentional step toward me, but I don't retreat.

"Reds do not retire," she repeats. "They kill or get killed."

"So who are we killing?"

Ruby sighs into me with her whole body. As if she can no longer stand on her own and she needs me to hold her upright. She turns her head to look up at me as she glides the tip of her dagger over my skin. It's a feather like touch, soft and deadly. Sensual. It makes my nerves go haywire and she knows it. She applies a hint of pressure, drawing beads of blood from my forearm.

"Cassius," she purrs. "Do you know what I love about you?"

I don't answer her, instead pressing my hard cock against her body so she can feel what she does to me.

A wicked grin flashes over her face. "I love that the threat of harm turns you on."

She presses the tip of her blade to the side of my throat, puncturing the skin. My dick pulses with need as I lift her from the ground. Her legs wrap around my torso as I pull her lips to mine. She bites me, and I pull away, the taste of iron filling my mouth.

A glint of silver flashes before my eyes, and for a second, I think the darkness is playing a trick on me. Her breath stills, and I know it's too late. I realize my mistake.

Her legs unhook from my body, and she steps back. Out of instinct, I put one hand on my throat, feeling my pulse as it bleeds between my fingers, sticky and wet. I reach my other hand toward her, but she's faster than I am. Betrayal kicks me in the gut. My body feels heavy and my brain swirls in a multitude of circles and grainy memories. She tilts her head in that peculiar way, the one that makes her look more feral and less human.

She takes a step forward, but it's already too late. By the time I react, she's sheathing the dagger she just used to stab me between the ribs.

Thirty-Six

Cassius stumbles backwards and opens his mouth to speak, but can't form the words.

Neither can I.

This is how it was always supposed to go. There was never any other choice. Never any other outcome. Cassius gasps for breath, blood sputtering from his throat. No longer a strong, capable opponent. No longer a man worthy of being my king. He's only a pawn in someone else's game.

His body collapses in a display of awkward limbs. A puppet who lost his master. A man taking his last breath.

I squat next to his body, digging my heels into the gravel. Pressing two fingers to the side of his neck, I feel for a pulse before I make the call to the cleaners.

I don't wait for them to arrive. I don't want to watch them load Cassius' still warm body into the back of one of the vans. Watching that would be my undoing and a risk I can't take. I can't fall apart now.

The house is quiet, which is not unusual for this time of night, but it's oddly bright. As if a flutter of activity ceased abruptly. I find Rowan in my bedroom, sitting cross-legged on my bed.

"Cleaners all set?" I ask her.

"Yes, and video evidence has been sent to the high court."

"Good, that buys me just enough time."

"Are you sure you have to go, Rubes?" she pleads with me. Her voice so small and child-like, it makes me pause.

"Come with me Row, we deserve more than this." I spread my arms indicating the Reds.

"Oh boy, where are we going, Rubes?" a voice from behind me taunts.

I turn to look at Rawlings who has her back leaning against my closed door.

"You know, Reagan figured something was up, but she couldn't seem to put her finger on what."

"Excuse me?" I say.

"You two," she gestures to Rowan and me, "were being more secretive than normal, and it was taking so long for Cassius to die, she got suspicious. She went to his club, you know?"

I did not know.

"She went for a job interview, and instead of letting her seduce him, he yelled at her and told her to never step foot in his club again. That's how she knew you were fucking him. So she started paying closer attention and then finally went to the high court with her proof. I don't think she imagined the ripple effect it would cause."

I bare my teeth at her, ready to pounce.

"Welp, anyway. Just want to let you know that I took care of it. Reagan will never snitch again." Rawlings smiles and mimes slicing her own throat.

One down, seven to go.

Rawlings was never the brightest. What kind of moron closes herself in a room with one of the deadliest women alive after fucking her over? She just made my night that much easier.

I laugh, I can't help it. I'm doubled over in laughter when a boot connects with my jaw, spraying blood across the floor. Using my crouched stance to my advantage, I swing my leg out, taking out both of hers. She jumps to her feet at the same time I pull a blade from the sheath on my side. We circle each other like two fighters in a cage. My strength has never been in combat, and there lies my disadvantage.

I twirl the dagger in my hand. She would be incredibly stupid to come within swiping distance and judging by the space she put between us, she knows it. With my other hand, I gesture to her in a come-hither motion.

"Let me see what all the fuss is about, Sophie. You aren't scared of a measly little dagger, are you?"

Her jaw clenches at my use of her real name. A sore subject, I suppose, like it is for most of us.

"I can see why you didn't want to take Cassius on yourself," I taunt. "He would have put a bullet between your eyes before you made your first move."

Sophie lunges at me, her emotions besting her. Her fist pulls back to land a punch, but my dagger presses into her kidney. One hand on her side, she attempts to stop the blood that's soaking through her shirt and spilling on my floor. I put a hand on my hip and tap my foot while I wait for her to stand upright again.

"You know Hannah's death wasn't Cassius' fault, right?" I ask. "It was your Daddy's fault. He pissed off the wrong people, and Cassius was just caught in the middle." Sophie's eyes widen, and I motion to Rowan still sitting on my bed, "She uncovered it earlier today, your Daddy's dirty business dealings. It was his fault, Sophie. Daddy dearest wasn't the man you thought he was."

She grits her teeth; her breath is heavy. Heavy enough that the sound fills the room. Sophie's body clenches in preparation, her shoulder drops, and I don't have time to prepare for the hit I take. My body is thrown backwards, my back hitting the footboard of my bed. Rowan screams. I close my eyes briefly, knowing I'm out of time. I wanted to play with Sophie. I wanted to dismember her and leave her in pieces around the compound, but now there's no time for that. Rowan's scream effectively put the entire compound on alert. I have roughly eight seconds before someone breaks down the door.

I remove a throwing dagger from my boot and flick it in

Sophie's direction. It enters her left eye with ease. I fist the other dagger and shove the blade upward at the underside of her jaw. The saw tooth on the back side of the dagger gets caught on muscle on the way back out, leaving pieces of skin hanging from the metal. I remove the throwing dagger from her eye, and it makes an odd popping sound that echoes in the room.

My bedroom door crashes to the floor, but I don't pause to see who enters. Everyone dies now. One by one, every person who dares to cross me will meet their maker. I am done living by rules.

Do not fuck with a queen, for she will die to protect what's hers.

More bodies enter, but I am in my zone. Daggers and throwing stars fly from my fingers, finding soft tissue and disarming those who enter just enough that I'm able to slide my blade across every throat. Empty eyes litter my floor. Gargled last words mingle with the scent of iron in the air.

Rowan looks so small still sitting on my bed, a little girl in an empty world.

"Row, we have to leave," I say softly, afraid to break the spell she's under, but also knowing it has to be done. I tread lightly. "You have to come. We're going to start over. You and me. But we have to go now before the high court gets wind of this." I gesture to the bodies at my feet.

"I..." she starts. "In all these years... I've never..." She looks at me then. "I've never seen this in person."

I reach for her hand. "Come on, Row, we have to leave."

I planned on killing them all, but not in this type of massacre. I planned to do it quietly to avoid alarming the little girls, the only people in this compound other than Rowan I will not kill. The appearance by Rawlings was not expected, and I should have known better. I should have had other plans in place in case things went sideways. But I didn't, Rowan screamed, and now here we are.

"But Ruby, I don't want to go. Besides, what about the girls?" Concern for the young recruits pulls at her features.

Riley's words float back to me.

Unless you do, and Ruby, I'd stand behind you on that.

"Riley isn't here," I tell Rowan gesturing to the mess of bodies at my feet. "She's with the girls, she'll take care of them." And I know in my heart that she will, that she meant what she said. "And because she sleeps in the dormitory with the girls, the high court will never know she's a sympathizer. She'll protect them as long as they need it. I know you don't want to go, but Row, if you don't come with me, the high court will kill you. You cannot die." Tears fill my eyes, and fear for the safety of my only friend spurs me into action. Grabbing her face in my hands, I force her to look at me. "I love you. Please, we need to go."

She stands and it strikes me what magic those words wield. I do love Rowan. I have loved her forever; I just didn't know what it meant to love until Cassius. Until he showed me that you can know someone's worst secrets and still love the person they are.

Rowan and I act fast. I grab whatever weapons I can carry on my person while keeping my hands free. Rowan stomps on our phones and pulls out the SIM cards, impaling them with one of the daggers scattered on the floor. Destroying evidence.

"I'll wipe everything else remotely," she tells me after I ask about the main systems.

We pause at the door, and I listen for movement, for the shuffle of small feet coming to investigate. The emptiness is eerie, but we don't have time to waste. I keep Rowan close to me as we walk along the hall. When the door finally closes behind us and the night air touches our faces, we both breathe a sigh of relief.

"You ready?" I ask her so quietly, I'm surprised she can hear me. Rowan nods in response.

We enter the woods to the east of the compound next to a small oak sapling where Rowan created a blind spot for the camera earlier tonight. We navigate the bare woods by moonlight until eventually it's too dark, and we're forced to turn on our lone flashlight. Rowan carries it, leaving the beam low to avoid possible detection. I need my hands free just in case. A snap of twigs behind us makes us both spin, but nothing is there.

"It was nothing, the woods like to play tricks at night. Besides," I reassure Rowan as much as myself, "everyone who would come after us is dead. But we do need to move faster," I tell her, nudging her in the back. We start to run, no longer worried about alerting anyone to our presence. None of it will matter if we're late. It will all have been for nothing. Tears sting at the backs of my eyes, already grieving the what if.

Rowan comes to a stop ahead of me and doubles over.

"Row!" I yell, but she waves me off.

"Just a cramp, Rubes, I'm good. But look." She points in the distance where we can see lights through the trees. I mirror her grin, and we take off again in the direction of the lights.

My shins ache and my chest burns, but I push because my future is just ahead. I can see it beyond the trees, beyond the fence that separates us. Beyond the veil of right and wrong.

When we finally reach the fence, I laugh with relief. Rowan climbs through first and I follow. As soon as both of our feet hit the tarmac, she pulls me in for a hug. The plane sits idling just a hundred yards away. We approach cautiously, because even though it's my plane, we can't be sure it hasn't been compromised. It feels like time is standing still. The air still, the world quiet. Everyone and everything paused with me in slow motion, wishing I could fast-forward. Have time on my side.

When we're only steps away from the stairs to the plane, the world unmutes itself. I hear yelling and sounds of a struggle and then...him. I try to call out, but cold steel presses against my neck, and warmth trickles in contrast with the cold, flowing down the trail between my breasts. A gunshot echoes through the night and it's then that I succumb to the darkness that has blanketed me my entire life.

THIRTY-SEVEN

I shoot. Her body falls. Rowan screams.

I shoot. Her body falls. Rowan screams.

I shoot. Her body falls. Rowan screams.

It plays over and over in my head. A never-ending time loop that I can't escape.

I thought I missed. For just a fraction of a second, but it was enough.

She dropped and my heart stopped.

Collectively, Garrett, Rowan, and I think shock played a factor. Fortunately, her wound was superficial, and we stopped the bleeding and patched Ember up, keeping to the strict schedule she was so intent on. Currently, we are in the air on our way to an unknown destination that even G and

Rowan don't know.

Ember shifts next to me in the bed at the back of the plane. When I lift my eyes to hers, they're open.

"I should kill you," I say. "To be fair, I probably should have killed you in the fucking alley. Then we could have avoided this entire mess. I could have avoided this." I touch my fingers to the bandage at my throat. "You almost killed me."

"I did kill you," she says softly, her voice scratchy with sleep and fatigue. "I didn't have a choice. It had to look as real as possible."

"You could have filled me in."

"The pain in your eyes had to be real. They would have known."

"I trusted you."

Tears well in her eyes. "I know, and I'm so sorry."

"How am I supposed to trust you again?"

She shrugs and smiles. "You can't kill a dead man."

"Did you just make a joke?" I laugh.

"Love has done crazier things."

"Is that what this is?" I ask her, pressing my lips to hers and then pulling away. "Love?"

She angles her head in that peculiar way she does that I fucking love. "A queen will stop at nothing to protect her king, even if it means massacring her own court and abandoning her kingdom."

I kiss her deep and slow, my tongue diving into her mouth. Her hands move to my chest, pulling me closer. I pull away, extracting myself from her grip.

"I need to be inside you. Now," I say, shedding my

clothes as she does the same.

I don't wait. I don't waste time on foreplay, we have the rest of our lives for that. Right now, I need to claim her. I need her to know she's mine. Carnal urge rages inside my veins, and by the time I enter her with a forceful grunt, I'm overcome with so much need that I barely register the soft "oh" that escapes her lips.

I pull out and slam back into her. She bites her lip, her eyes hooded with her own desire. This is a claiming. She. Is. Mine. I thrust hard and deep, her hips pressing up to meet mine. I tease her nipple with my teeth, pulling it until she yelps. Her nails scratch down my back and it takes every ounce of self-control I have not to bang on my chest like a fucking caveman. My dick throbs. I'm hard as stone pounding into her tight cunt over and over again.

"You. Are. Everything," I say between thrusts.

"Cassius," she moans. My name on her lips as her pussy squeezes the head of my cock is one of the hottest fucking things I've ever experienced. I pull out completely, and she whines as if the loss of me is too much. She wraps her legs around my waist, locking her ankles and pulling me back to her. I glide the head of my cock over her entrance, and she squeezes me tighter, forcing me inside. Leaning back, I lift her hips off the bed, angling myself deeper, aligning myself to that spot she likes. My balls tap her ass with each thrust, and I find her clit with one hand, rubbing gently at first. Then faster, harder.

"Be a good queen and come on your king's cock, baby."

As I say the words, I pinch her clit. Her legs tighten around me, forcing me still, and her cunt squeezes me, a vice grip on my dick. Warm juices explode on my cock, and her legs loosen, the sweetest cry leaving her lips.

We flip over, and her nails dig into my chest as she rides me, impaling herself on my hard shaft. She rolls her hips, her pussy doing things to me that I didn't think were possible. Her tits bounce, and I push myself to my elbows, so I can bury my face between them. She tugs at my hair as she finds a position she likes.

Pulling back, I look her in the eye. "Take it baby, take what's yours."

Her hips thrust faster and faster. My hands dig into her sides, pushing her to find that rhythm I know will finish us both. Her eyes meet mine when it happens, that feeling of euphoria building in both of us.

"You are mine," she says softly and then her pussy tightens, and we both explode.

Together. Always.

Because we're playing for keeps.

EPILOGUE: SIX MONTHS LATER

C assius uses his Smith and Wesson to scratch his temple before speaking. "Babe, I thought these high court queens were supposed to be the best of the best?"

"Clearly not," I reply, gesturing to the Ruby from England tied to a chair between us. "Because otherwise this old bitch would have found a better place to hide after we killed the rest of them."

Ruby, or rather Sarah, as she was once called, tries to speak, but the sound is muffled by the gag in her mouth. She is the last standing Ruby. I saved her for last because in a way, I have her to thank for introducing me to Cassius.

"To be fair," I continue, "she was the hardest to find. It took us, what? A month?"

Cassius places his gun on the table, trading it for one that shoots staples instead of bullets.

"Yeah, but only because G and Row have been a bit distracted." Cassius hits me with a cocked eyebrow.

I laugh because he's right. That was something I certainly didn't see coming.

Sarah turns her head, shifting between me and Cassius, like she's trying to solve a puzzle but can't see what she's looking at.

"Ah, babe," Cassius crows. "She really did think I was dead. You did such a good job." He pulls me to his side and kisses my hair, then steps forward to remove the gag.

"But ... but," Sarah sputters. "You? Both of you?"

"You see, you old fucking cunt, unlike you, my girl here really is the fucking best."

Cassius puts a staple in her little toes. Screams vibrate off the concrete walls, and he lets them die off before he continues.

And this is the part I love. The part where Cassius tells our story. Between a sleeve of staples and screams, he tells her of our first meeting, including that dribble of cum. He never seems to omit that part. He tells her about the alley and how the speck of blood on my face turned him on. How he knew he loved me in that picture she saw of me in his shirt. He shows her his scars, the ones I gave him before we fucked for the first time. He tells her how he held me after I killed my parents. And how bad it hurt when he thought I betrayed him.

Which is where he puts down the staple gun, and I grab my dagger and finish the story.

"You know one of the greatest perks about being Ruby?" I ask her, not bothering to wait for an answer. "The fucking money." I slide the blade across her cheek, digging into the soft flesh. "I don't really have an explanation for why I thought I might need the cleaners one day, but I guess I thought I could buy their loyalty." Laughter bubbles in my throat. "And you know what? I did. Every job they cleaned up for me, they made an extra twenty percent."

Twirling my dagger around my finger, I circle Sarah. "And do you know what that twenty percent did? It saved—"

"Fuck you!" Sarah spits. "You will die for this." Cassius hands me the gag, and I shove it back into her mouth.

"Tsk-tsk, Sarah, it's rude to interrupt people." She winces at the use of her birth name, and I thrust my dagger into her thigh. Blood gurgles out of the wound as I pull it out and watch as she slowly bleeds out.

"Anyway," I continue, "that twenty percent saved Cassius, along with some impressive sleight of hand, a heavy dose of morphine, and some fake blood."

Sarah's head starts to slump down, and I slap her across the face.

"You don't get to die yet," I tell her. "I'm not done with my part of the story."

Cassius hands me a crafting knife, and I begin my carving in Sarah's back.

"You see, the cleaners picked up Garrett, Cassius' best friend, on their way to the air strip with an unconscious Cassius. Rowan, the genius that she is, had been able to get a message to Garrett with instructions. And while they were waiting for us, I went back to the house, and well you know what happened there."

I carve an X and hand the knife to Cassius. He carves an

O in the upper right corner of the grid.

Sarah slumps down, but Cassius forces her head upright again before giving me back the knife.

"Basically, I killed all the Reds."

I carve an X and return the knife to Cassius, who says, "Except for Riley, and the little girls. That part's important."

"Right, except for Riley and the girls. So, all the Reds are dead except for me, Rowan, Riley, and the girls. Rowan and I left through the front door, and we walked through the woods to the airstrip to meet Cassius and Garrett. We made it onto the tarmac, and we weren't far from the plane when I heard Cassius yelling. Then I saw his face as he walked onto the stairs of the plane."

I pause to ponder Cassius' move before making one of my own and returning the knife to him. Stepping in front of Sarah, I glide my dagger across her other cheek, matching the first.

"Then there was steel at my throat and blood trickling down my neck. That's the last thing I remember."

Cassius slides the crafting knife back into my palm, and I take a look at our game. The winning spot is open, just like always. I mark it with my X.

"I shot her. The little girl, Alice," Cassius says the same way he always does, with a throat full of grief, but a heart full of love. "For a minute I thought I missed and shot Ember because Rowan screamed, and Ember crumbled to the ground. And the girl, she just stood there for a split second before she fell too."

I sigh. "We were never queens. We were all just pawns in a bigger game, following someone else's rules and doing the bidding of others. And Alice? She really was going to be a better Ruby than me, but she, like the rest of you, would have never had that one thing that makes me the best. Love. It's because of that love that I know what it really means to be queen. You see, a queen is the most powerful piece on the board, she moves without limits, without fear. She is the protector. The muscle. But what the Reds failed to teach us is that the queen is only powerful if she has a king to protect. Without him, she loses the game. And my king? He's a good fucking shot."

Sarah's eyes narrow in pain, and her head starts to fall again, but Cassius stands behind her and holds her head so she can look me in the eye. My blade glides swiftly across her throat. Due to her leg wound, the blood splatter is minimal, but I watch as her eyes roll back. I hold my breath until she takes her last.

Then I douse the body, the basement, and the entire first floor of the house in gasoline. When we get outside, Cassius holds me close and presses his lips to mine.

"I love you," I say when he pulls away.

"I love you too," he replies and hands me the matchbook.

I light a single match before lighting the entire book on fire. Then I throw it through the front door, and we watch as the fire comes to life. It dances in the dark night, hot and wild. Hungry and impatient.

Cassius takes my hand and together we turn our backs on the flames, having successfully flipped the board on the Reds...

Checkmate.

Acknowledgements

Special thanks to the people who have supported me on this long journey.

To my amazing husband, who has always been my biggest fan. Thank you for listening to me plot out loud, and putting up with having a laptop in our bed.

To my kids for being proud of me, even though I wrote a "weird sex book".

To my mom, for instilling my love of books, even the creepy ones. And my dad for always keeping at least a handful of Stephen King novels in the house. Thank you for writing notes to the librarians, so I could check out Fear Street books when all of my friends were reading Goosebumps.

To Cupcake and Dree, who have literally been there for me from the first line. Thank you for reading chapter after chapter of utter crap, and hyping me up when I wanted to quit.

To Kelly for adopting me (a complete stranger) as a new author and friend. You have been my sounding board since I typed "The End" and I greatly appreciate all the help and advice you've offered. And to Mel for not only introducing me, but also for supporting my craziness.

To my eighth grade English teacher, who I hope never reads this book, for encouraging us to think outside the box, and to enjoy our life, not just live in it. All these years later, I'm sad to say I still haven't golfed with friends just for fun, but I did write a book!

To my beta readers, I appreciate all of your feedback. Your criticism and praise will only make me a better writer.

To Utterly Unashamed editing, thank you for forcing me to add contractions when I really didn't want to, but you were right. It didn't flow right without them.

To Gigi's Creatives for putting into art what I couldn't. This cover is everything I wanted.

About the Author

Jess Allen has been an avid reader since childhood, and has been dabbling in creative writing just as long. Bleeding Outside the Lines is her debut novel.

Jess lives in Massachusetts with her husband, two sons and two dogs. When she isn't writing, she enjoys annoying the shit out of her husband, camping or attempting to tackle her TBR.

She loves a good true-crime documentary and may be a tad obsessed with Veronica Mars and Gilmore Girls (#teamloganX2)

Made in the USA
Middletown, DE
06 September 2024